Future Dawning

or

Awakening in America

(A Spiritual Fantasia on World Themes)

by

Glen Williamson

(for Dr. James Dyson)

a drama in two parts
in sequel to
the four mystery dramas by and through
Rudolf Steiner
(and in appreciation of Tony Kushner's
Angels in America)

Cover art:
Painting by Sophie Bourguignon Takada
Calendar of the Soul, Twenty-Eighth Week

PREFACE

In February 2010, my friend Dr. James Dyson and I had a conversation in JFK airport about the need for new and future mystery dramas. It has been my lifelong quest to find and create theater with spiritual substance, and I had recently co-authored and begun performing *Aeschylus Unbound*. The idea arose between us that someone might perhaps create a drama about Rudolf Steiner's mystery drama characters in their next incarnation. Sometime later, in the summer of 2010, on the island of Tiree, in Scotland, James specifically asked (requested) me to write such a drama. I soberly agreed. With intense, heartfelt feeling and emotion, he acknowledged his deep longing for drama as a container for the new medical mysteries.

I began imagining, a little bit each day, like watering a growing plant, drawing from Goethe's fairytale, from history, from observations and experience, as well as from Steiner and other playwrights. I shared thoughts and characters and storylines with James now and then, but mostly I was on my own. In the summer of 2012, while camping with my partner in Maine, I committed to an outline of eleven scenes, beginning with many characters at a funeral, going through a retrospective of the twentieth century incarnation, entering spirit realms and ending in a temple. (James and I had had a tremendous amount of struggle and a long conversation, near Eleusis in Greece, about whether that temple would be on earth or in the spiritual world.) Then, the next eleven mornings, before hiking or swimming, I drafted dialogue for one scene each day. (I'm not sure I would recommend this approach, but I felt I had to give myself a deadline to get something down on paper.) I wrote by hand and only later typed it into my computer. I was able to show a full rough draft to James when we crossed paths in London in September. He seemed to be very moved by it, and that encouraged me. I continued struggling inwardly with themes and characters. In June 2013, on a beach in Ireland, James, David Fairclough (to whom I owe the title "Future Dawning") and I read through the two-act draft together.

While I was immersed in rehearsals for all four of Steiner's plays in Spring Valley, I had some time and quiet space to tinker and to write and form some scenes, especially the final Temple scene. I gave myself a deadline of Epiphany, 2015, to finish a second draft. The scene in Ahriman's realm came together during a few quiet days of grace in Camphill California before Christmas. In January, I shared the play with seven trusted friends, including James and David. Their responses and suggestions were encouraging and helpful. I kept working and set aside the month of April for substantial revisions. I barely met the deadline for a reading with a group of friends at the Christian Community in Spring Valley in July, 2015 (even adding a short scene at the last minute before printing). John Alexandra, with James, organized the reading, and David Fairclough, Barbara Renold, Laurie Portocarrero, Marke Levene, Franz Eilers, Brigida Baldszun, Bella Freuman also generously participated. The six-hour, 25-scene play seemed to be engaging (people didn't want to stop reading). I was willing and happy to be finished with the project and had no expectation that anyone would want to do anything further with such a thing. But there was a strong will among several people present to organize a public staged reading of *Future Dawning* and Marke Levene's and Michael Burton's *The Working of the Spirit* in a common event. So I committed myself to further work. Problems and needed revisions became clear through conversations the next day and beyond. One plotline in particular required considerable pondering and struggle over the next months. Five and a half years after James' request, the final revisions seem to be complete, and I now can call the script finished. The readings of the two plays are scheduled for Whitsun weekend, May 14 and 15, in Fountain Hall in Camphill USA in Copake, New York. I am looking forward to experiencing *The Working of the Spirit*, which I have not yet read, so as not to be influenced by it.

I have tried to be true to the characters and their further development, but I have not tried to write or imagine what Rudolf Steiner may have envisioned for further dramas (though I think that would be a valuable exercise). Instead, I wanted to write something surprising and unpredictable out of my own perception of the world. So I have included several themes – three, I think – that may be controversial, themes that Steiner didn't elaborate – at least not explicitly . . . at least not in the early-twentieth-century incarnation of his characters. I also originally intended not to imitate Steiner's style of verse, but to develop a free poetic style of my own, inspired by other playwrights. However, I soon found myself drawn into iambic verse, often pentameter. And, surprisingly to me, this imitation of Steiner-in-English-translation turned out to be the most effective and engaging approach. Even many sections where I deliberately attempted a more colloquial, naturalistic style had to be elevated into verse. A few of these more colloquial sections remain, but the overall style, variable though it may be, is more consistent than I had originally intended. I have however, been freer with the verse form than Steiner is. (His iambic pentameter becomes increasingly regular.) I have borrowed not only from Steiner's dramas and their fragments and sketches, but also from some of his lectures, verses and letters, transposing vocabulary, phrases and even whole speeches and scenes into new situations and characters. I've often carefully considered and retranslated the original German, but have also relied on Hans and Ruth Pusch and consulted Adam Bittleston, Harry Collison, Alexander Gifford, Richard Ramsbotham and Michael Hedley Burton and Adrian Locher.

Besides Steiner and Goethe, Novalis (*Hymn VII*), Tony Kushner, Vladimir Solovyov, Johanna Gräfin Keyserlingk, Aeschylus, Dante via T.S. Elliot, Shakespeare, Dostoyevsky, Lincoln, Shelter Somerset and Hiram Bingham have also been sources of inspiration, language, themes, images and situations.

A note on Tony Kushner's *Angels in America*: although its social-political message can be overpowering, I am not aware of any other popular modern drama – since Dickens or Thornton Wilder – that so boldly crosses the threshold into soul-spiritual experiences. So I wanted *Future Dawning* to also be a response and tribute to *Angels in America*. However, I soon discovered that Kushner's rambunctious poetic style and wonderfully anachronistic humor and irony, even if I were capable of something similar, would not be appropriate for this assignment.

When we read, play or watch Rudolf Steiner's mystery dramas, we know that they were written by a great initiate and so we look for and experience deep wisdom within each word and moment and situation. In order to write a mystery drama, one has to have a much more comprehensive clarity about what is true than do other playwrights. Where my vision falls short, I have had to rely on Steiner or guess and imagine. Of course I would like to think that I have also been inspired and helped by beings in the spiritual world, so that audiences and readers will experience something more, speaking through this play, than I have been conscious of. In any case, if I have depicted or implied something that is spiritually untrue or misleading, I trust that it will do no harm, since people know that this play is not written by a great initiate. Although it seems to have evolved into a somewhat coherent (and very large) whole (which was, after all, the goal) this project has been for me a kind of sketchbook of experiments and exercises. How much of what Rudolf Steiner was trying to express in his dramas really lives in me as my own knowledge and experience? Writing *Future Dawning* has confronted me with that wonderful and terrible question. It seems worth noting that whenever I dictate the title "Future Dawning" to the voice recognition on my smart phone, what gets transcribed is "future daunting".

I have studied, watched, read and acted in Steiner's dramas many times over the years. I have gotten to know them in a different way through this playwriting process. And I would highly recommend it. At times I have felt that I was coming close to what Steiner may have experienced in forming scenes, characters, situations, language and verse. At other times I know I have worked on this project in a very different, perhaps more conventional, way. Becoming aware of and struggling with that difference has been an extremely valuable experience. Whether the results will be engaging to readers or audiences, and whether that engagement will at moments even begin to approach the depths of engagement we experience (admittedly, with a lot of effort) with Steiner's dramas, remains to be seen. If Future Dawning begins to awaken our capacity to perceive and experience this difference in levels of playwriting, then – I can't help quoting Johannes Thomasius – I have done the service that I had in mind. As a work of art I do not rate it highly.

I have said very little here about the content of the play. Although The Bridge of Christ has certain similarities to several religious and spiritual movements, it is my own invention, for which I take full responsibility. Other similarities in *Future Dawning* to historic persons, places and events, past, present and future, although perhaps intentional, are also fictional. Events in this drama should be taken not as what did happen, is happening or will happen, but as what could happen in a fictional parallel reality that is a continuation of the historical fictional world of Steiner's dramas. Beyond that I will let the play speak for itself.

Finally, I have to say that I am profoundly grateful to my friend James for embarking me on this harrowing journey. Of course we know that working together creatively, reading, acting in and producing Rudolf Steiner's mystery dramas is a very fruitful path. Who would have known that such a valuable probation could also be found in attempting to write one? I hope (and I know Marke Levene shares this hope) that more and more people will attempt such things in the future.

GW
NYC
February, 2016

*In her next life . . . she will be an occultist
and on request tell people their past lives
clear back to the beginning of the earth.*

– Ahriman, of Maria Treufels,
Guardian of the Threshold, Scene 8.

CHARACTERS

ROBERT FINN
> Schoolteacher, storyteller and puppeteer. Married to Barbara Finn. One of his hands is withered or mis-shapen or missing. Age thirty.

BARBARA ("BOBBY") FINN
> Biodynamic gardener and dairy farmer. Married to Robert Finn. Late twenties.

CHILD
> of Barbara and Robert Finn. Appears only in the last scene. Three years old.

SPIRIT OF BENEDICTUS
> Spiritual teacher and clairvoyant spirit researcher in the early 20th Century.

SPIRIT OF STELLA SOPHIA
> Founder of the community, farm, school (and therapeutic center) where the Finns are active and where Joanna and Troy (and Marcus, for a few years) went to school. (She died shortly before the play begins, aged well over 100). She speaks with a thick German accent.

TRAUTA S. HARRIS
> High level philosopher-bureaucrat in the Cultural Authority of the world government.

FOUR DENIZENS OF THE SOPHIA COMMUNITY

SETTING
A community in the Northeast of North America; a church in the Midwest; the Monument and Archives of the work of Benedictus in Central Europe; various etheric, soul and spiritual realms.

TIME
The not-too-distant future and, in retrospect, the early 20th Century.

Part One
Time Approaching

PRELUDE
A room in Tom and Mary's house.

ACT I (Scenes 1 – 4)
1) The Sophia Community, the Northeast of North America
2) A government office
3) Sophia Community and the Midwest
4) Church of The Bridge of Christ in the Midwest

ACT II
5) The Sophia Community
6) Landscape in the Midwest
7) Ahriman's Realm

ACT III
8) A cafe
9) Church of The Bridge of Christ
10) An apartment in the Midwest

ACT IV
11) Church of The Bridge of Christ
12) The Temple Monument and Archives, Europe
13) Church of The Bridge of Christ

Prelude

(A room in Tom and Mary's house. Mary and Tom and their two children, a boy and a girl.)

THE CHILDREN *(sing – music by Merwin Lewis, verse by Rudolf Steiner. Tom accompanies them on a lyre or recorder.)*

> The plant seed are quickened in the night of the earth,
> the green herbs are sprouting in the might of the air
> and all fruits are ripened in the power of the sun.
> So quickens the soul in the shrine of the heart,
> so blossoms spirit power in the light of the world,
> so ripens spirit strength in the glory of God.

TOM
Now go to your room, children, and think about the words we have been singing.
(Tom and Mary lead the Children to the door to their rooms.)

MARY
Goodbye, dear, I'm off to the performance of that new mystery drama that our Branch is hosting in the auditorium tonight.

TOM
Oh yes – that slipped my mind. I was hoping you would be here for our study group tonight. We are reading "The Souls' Awakening" and we were hoping you would take a major role.

MARY
I'm sorry dear. But I've been looking forward to this production for so long.

TOM
I was rejoicing with all my heart at the thought of having you beside me. These dramas are so deep and complex. The real depths of spiritual science are contained in them. In fact, I think that they reveal profound truths and realities that Steiner didn't speak or write about anywhere else. And when you really work your way into them, you realize that they are the wildest dramas ever written.

MARY

Yes, I know dear. I love those dramas as much as you do. I also think it's time for us to develop something new and not only depend on what Rudolf Steiner has given us. Tonight's production is an attempt at that.

TOM

Yes. I've heard it is a kind of sequel to Steiner's four dramas, a "Fifth Mystery Drama."

MARY

Actually, it is a kind of seventh drama – his characters in their next incarnation.

TOM

– in a fictional world in the near future with a fictional church, a fictional spiritual community and a fictional world government, none of which, despite some similarities, ever existed in Steiner's plays or in the real world. I just think it's presumptuous and superficial for anyone to attempt such a thing.

MARY

Obviously this play was not written by an initiate. So people in the audience are free to decide for themselves whether it reveals any spiritual realities or just the personal opinions of the author.

TOM

But that's just it. How could anyone dare to write a so-called "mystery drama" who doesn't have the necessary credentials, so to speak, the esoteric chops.

MARY

But if we wait until an equally great initiate comes along, or until Rudolf Steiner himself appears again and writes more plays, then it won't ever happen. If we never try to do what is beyond our present capabilities, then how will we progress? Perhaps by attempting the impossible, we can develop capacities that in the future will bear fruit.

TOM
That is all well and good.   But why should audiences, or these producers, actors and directors in our circles, indulge and give so much attention to something that is only the attempt of a mere dabbler speculating about the laws of karma and the spirit realms, which he can't possible understand, at least not with anything approaching the perception and insight of a great initiate. We have four dramas Rudolf Steiner wrote. And they contain enough to occupy our mind and soul for many years and even lifetimes. I see no point in making other dramas.

MARY
I understand your point of view. And I do wish I could also be with you tonight to work together with our friends on Steiner's dramas.

TOM
And I do hope that you find tonight's production somehow enriching.
I will be interested to hear about it.

MARY
When I come back here afterward, we will find each other again.
I must go.

TOM
Goodbye now!

(End of scene.)

Act One

1) Last of the Mohicans

(A beautiful auditorium or meeting hall. The stage is filled with the warm glow of candle light. A solemn, sacred atmosphere prevails. Someone is playing the harp music. Robert Finn, Marcus Lilly, Barbara Finn, Simon and Celia Stratham, Joanna and the four denizens are all present, perhaps seated in the audience. There is a photograph or painting of Stella Sophia by which we are able to recognize her when her soul appears.)

ROBERT FINN *(After the Harp music ends.)*
How beautiful. We know how Miss
Sophia loved to listen to the harp.
She'd often sing its lovely melodies.

And now, we're blessed and comforted
to welcome here from Europe, Marcus Lilly
who heads the Temple Monument and Archives.

MARCUS
(He speaks with a slight central European accent, perhaps German or Swiss, but is fluent in American English.)
Dear friends, my heart is grieving with you
to see you ailing in your soul and spirit
at this significant moment
when so much change comes toward you and our movement.
I thought that I had come to you today
to honor and remember Miss Sophia,
who was my teacher when I came to school here,
and then my friend and mentor ever since.
The last remaining pupil of our leader
Benedictus, –
has now departed from the earth.
No one is left who heard him speak, that great
initiate and scientist of spirit;
no one who walked with him and met his gaze
or saw his gestures and his light-filled deeds.

Our dear Stella Sophia was the last.
While still a child, she sat upon his lap.
She heard his teachings from his very lips.
She stood among the people watching as
the Temple of the Word went up in flames.
She brought that Temple's wisdom here
and founded this community
and it has flourished. – –
If it were not for her you would not be here.
But now I find I must address what weighs
so urgently on you in recent days,
what Miss Sophia has been spared from witnessing,
since she departed in the night before
the government investigators came.
I cannot read the plan laid out to guide the earth,
and yet I know that everything
that comes to meet us has a meaning.
As we remember our dear Miss Sophia,
it seems no accident that at this moment
the circle of her friends and neighbors here
is being challenged. – I have no doubt
that she would want you now to summon all
your heartfelt striving and your inner strength
to come to better understanding with
the world leaders you have long supported.
She could express a knowledge of the spirit
in ways that common sense could grasp
and then apply to daily life.
As Miss Sophia would have done, we must
combine our deepest wisdom with good will
to work with the authorities and show
the regulations and requirements can be revised
and that your products and your ways of life
and education are exemplary.
The ways your children play are not unsafe.
Your food and medicines are good and wholesome.
And anyone can come to understand this.
There lived in Miss Sophia's heart
the glowing faith that

surely a time would come
uniting all humanity,
in brotherhood and sisterhood,
with equal access to the world's resources,
and freedoms not for just a few, but all.
What spirit science can reveal
about the wondrous nature of the universe
would pour forth happiness
from your creative work
into the hearts of humankind.
That's what she thought and hoped.
A future blessing in the form
of work that's practical, yet filled with beauty,
giving new meaning to all walks of life,
would spring forth from the working of the spirit
developed here in your community.
Thus Miss Sophia often
proclaimed for us our spirit's goal.
But now, the forces of our inner life are
shrouded by doubts and cares.
It almost seems that Miss Sophia's death
foretells a looming danger in the air.

(*Stella Sophia's Soul appears and gradually comes nearer Marcus Lilly from behind him.*)

Like a canary in a coal mine,
singing with joy – – –
until its death proclaims the air's unsafe,
she was not daunted by impending peril.
In gloomy times of dull and dead'ning cares
she could breathe cosmic air that quickens life.
I know that she is with us here in spirit.
If only we could hear what she would say. (*He pauses, falling into deep musing.*)

CELIA (*stands up*)
Excuse me, but I feel compelled to speak.
I see a loom of light, a radiant form.

Stella Sophia's spirit hovers near you
and, like an angel, speaks to us in warning.

STELLA SOPHIA'S SOUL (*Marcus does not see or hear her.*)
Our temple's held in darkness. Seek it out.
For it is yet unknown and still unseen.
The scattered seeds will not bear fruit,
till demons working in the depths of worlds
can sense what in your own true self is moved
to find and choose affinity with them –
and those who knowingly beheld
the heights of spirit from their depths of soul
can truly know each other once again.
The deeds of human destiny proclaim:
Disharmony of spirits can destroy
what each alone would like to bring about.
Dispersed, you will not find the sacred place,
which has been built for spirit realms
from substance of the suffering of souls.
For spirit life will vanish from the earth
unless the powers of vision waken you.

MARCUS (*coming out of his deep musing*)
What can you hear her saying to us now?

CELIA
She speaks of wak'ning to a sacred place.
Can you not hear her or perceive her presence?

MARCUS
Clear knowledge of the spirit is not open
to my perception and experience.
I am a dark enigma to myself.
When will the Temple rise again? Oh when
will life spring forth from the dead monument?
Forgive me. I have nothing more to say.
Stella Sophia, our friend, is no more.
Now, Robert Finn, please tell us of her life.

(Robert Finn steps onto the stage as we hear pounding on a door. Barbara Finn goes out. Voices are heard outside.)

ROBERT FINN
I can but speak in pictures and in stories,
and Miss Sophia's life has always seemed
to me to be a kind of Fairy Tale.
So that is all that I can offer here:
(He lights another candle.)
Once upon a time,
more than a hundred years ago,
there lived a wise and radiant woman,
devoted to the Spirit and to higher knowledge.
With her entire being she absorbed
the words of her great teacher, who
carried within his soul the love and wisdom
of all ages, reawakened for his and future times.
With warmth and discipline she carried out
the work he gave to guide her on the path
of inner life and spirit sight.
She often gathered many people
from varied walks of life
to listen to her teacher and converse
about the thoughts and practices
he shared from his great wisdom.
        One day a child appeared,
an infant on the woman's doorstep,
and try though she did,
she could not find out who the child's parents were.
The woman had no children of her own
and had no husband, so

(Barbara returns.)

BARBARA
Excuse me, Robert.
I'm sorry, but I have to interrupt.
Investigators are insisting that . . .

ROBERT
I know. We have to put the candles out.

BARBARA
No, not just that. We have to leave the Hall.
They are enforcing structure regulations
and closing this old building. We are not
allowed to meet here anymore. –
(*beat*)   Let's reconvene
at the reception in the school –
in half an hour, just across the road.

(*End of scene.*)

2) Speak Freely

(*A government office resembling a small courtroom. Trauta S. Harris
sits on the seat of judgment. Michael Capstone is present. Later, the
soul forces, the Other Philia, Astrid and Luna, appear.*)

TRAUTA HARRIS
(*Looking through a stack of forms and papers.*)
Incorporated, . . registered and licensed . . . .
Now Reverend Capstone . . May I call you Reverend
or is it "Father" Capstone I should call you?

MICHAEL CAPSTONE
"Michael" is fine. Or "Mr. Capstone". Either.
I do conduct the service, our Communion,
but I am not a "Father" or a priest.

TRAUTA HARRIS
And I am Agent Harris, Trauta S.
I serve the Cultural Authority.
I'm here to question you about your church.
What is the name of your religious movement?

CAPSTONE
It's called The Bridge of Christ.

TRAUTA HARRIS
                    How did it start?

CAPSTONE
Our New Communion ritual was received
from God in 1938 in England,
within a group of people some of whom
had come from Germany to Britain.

TRAUTA HARRIS
What are your principle activities?

CAPSTONE
We try to bring the work of Jesus Christ
to life and make it real for each of us,
sharing our sins and wrongs with one another,
surrendering our life into God's keeping,
making amends with all whom we have wronged
and list'ning to and car'ying out God's guidance.

TRAUTE HARRIS
Rrr-reverend Capstone, you have openly
resisted unifying principles
of the United Union's global laws.
Do you intend to still continue to
promote divisive ideologies?

CAPSTONE
We share experiences of Jesus Christ
and do our utmost to become true Christians.

TRAUTA HARRIS
Can you see how your ultra-Christian views
might be offensive to some other people.

CAPSTONE
Freedom of speech means some may feel offended.
How people feel is not a legal question.
At least it shouldn't be. – –

TRAUTA HARRIS
So you do not embrace the principles
of world inclusion and diversity.

CAPSTONE
Everyone is welcome in our church
and to participate in services.

TRAUTA HARRIS
What are your church's teachings and beliefs?

CAPSTONE
We have our meetings, prayers and principles.
We also read the Bible carefully
and share with one another what we think.

TRAUTA HARRIS
What *do* you think? And what do you believe?
Say, is the Bible literally true?

CAPSTONE
The Bible does reveal God's holy truth
through history and revelation.

TRAUTA HARRIS
Is it the word of God?

CAPSTONE
                    Our Lord and Savior,
Jesus the Christ himself's the Word of God.

TRAUTA HARRIS
And do you think that Jesus was divine?

CAPSTONE
Yes, fully God and fully human too.
For, in him, God and Man became one being.

TRAUTA HARRIS
Do you believe in so-called Virgin Birth?

CAPSTONE
The birth of Jesus is unique in history,
for Jesus Christ is God in Man, the
only-begotten and eternal son.
The Word came to be flesh and lived on earth.

TRAUTA HARRIS
When she gave birth, was Mary still a virgin?

CAPSTONE
Yes. She was virginal in soul and body.

TRAUTA HARRIS
And do you think that he rose from the dead?

CAPSTONE
Through death, the resurrected Jesus Christ
restored our broken bond with God and heaven
and made it possible for sinful man
to reunite at last with the divine.

TRAUTA HARRIS
This old idea of sin is now outdated,
dividing people into saints and sinners.
We now give equal benefits to all,
without distinction or discrimination.

CAPSTONE
The shepherd separates the sheep and goats.

(*beat*)

TRAUTA HARRIS
Do you teach evolution or creation?

CAPSTONE
I think that God created everything.
Darwinian theory *can* be a *deception*.

TRAUTA HARRIS
Did God create the world in six days?

CAPSTONE
Yes, then he rested on the Seventh Day.

TRAUTA HARRIS
What is your definition of a marriage?

CAPSTONE
Of marriage?

TRAUTA HARRIS
Yes, of marriage. Do you rec . . . (*She continues speaking, but we cannot hear her. Soul Forces, the Other Philia, Astrid and Luna, appear. They are portrayed in movement by eurythmists, their speakers offstage. Astrid is encumbered by chains or a dark veil.*)

THE OTHER PHILIA
Your soul is inflamed
with a thirst that is kindled
by the bearer of light,
who opens up worlds
of radiant beauty
and quickens your zeal
for the kingdom of God.

ASTRID
The temple is burning
with fire that is hungry
for cosmic foundations
of primeval worlds,
where an altar is hidden
and wisdom in love
is concealed from the heart.

LUNA
Defeat is collapsing
the feelings that dare
to fearlessly stand
in the craving of senses.
And danger encloses
the person abstaining
from deeds that would search
in realms where the secrets
of demons hold sway.

TRAUTA HARRIS
Uh, Reverend Capstone . . .

CAPSTONE
                Pardon me.

TRAUTA HARRIS
You were dissociated for a moment.
Now please provide your answer to the question:
What is your definition of a marriage?

CAPSTONE
A marriage is the sacred union of
a man and woman only, nothing else.

TRAUTA HARRIS
Our time is up. I think you've given us
all that we need for now about the "Bridge Church".

CAPSTONE
The Bridge of Christ. – – –

TRAUTA HARRIS
Well, thank you, Reverend Capstone. Your official
hearing will be tomorrow. You may go.

                (End of scene.)

3) Spilt Milk

(*Joanna Thomason and Troy Fels. Later, Barbara Finn. Joanna and Troy on opposite sides of the stage. Outside the auditorium of the Sophia Community, during the "break" at Stella Sophia's memorial, Joanna speaking on her mobile "dumb" phone. Somewhere in the Midwest, Troy speaks on his.*)

TROY
Oh, I am sorry I am missing that.
I love the way that Robert tells his stories.
Whenever I remember them
and call them up in my imagination,
I can enjoy them again
with all my heart.

JOANNA
Dear brother, your devotion to our spirit science
has often manifested in your love
of poetry and stories; and also in
the healing forces that pour out of
your vivid inner life and in your love for
the angels that our mother can perceive.

TROY
Our parents both arrived while I was there,
so I saw *them* before I left.

JOANNA
I'm sorry that I just missed seeing you.

TROY
Have you seen Marcus yet?

JOANNA
　　　　　　　　　He spoke just now.
Before the interruption. −　But
I haven't had a chance to say hello.
We all expected you would be here *with* him.

You are such opposites in many ways,
and yet you are his other half.

TROY
                        It's true.
For we were one in time's deep womb,
before the will of gods divided us
and we embarked on many lives on earth
and lost and found each other many times –
as different and alike as light and warmth.
His soul is my soul's higher sister.
But now we have to go our separate ways,
on our own quests toward spirit goals.
The love we share must now expand,
or it will die. – –
The warmth of love I have for him
is also healing power in the world.
I had to leave the Temple Monument:
for him it is the center of the world;
for me, the spirit air's too cold there and
I cannot breath. – –
So I came back to North America.

JOANNA
Oh Troy, my dearest brother,
so often in our lives,
I've seen how your soul's inner life
has been reflected in my own.
My longing for your soulmate, Marcus,
has been unwavering,
though destiny's necessity
has led me to stand faithfully
at my late husband's side.
I could not find the way to reach your soulmate,
as long as in my heart the warmth of love
would not give way unto the light of love.
And if you sacrifice *your* warmth of love
for spirit work, then you may find the way
to reach him once again.
Your healing work in medicine will guide you.

TROY
I am conferring with some nurses here
and doctors.
And I am on a quest,
a certain inner calling in my heart
I have to follow.
But since you've come half way around the world
and I have now returned from Europe,
we really have to find a way
to have a conversation face to face
while we're both on this continent.
I know that you'll be here next month,
signing your books, all over the Midwest.
Do you think we could get together then?

JOANNA
Yes. Troy, that would be wonderful.

TROY
Hello?

JOANNA
     That would be wonderful.

TROY
                          Joanna,
Hey, can you hear me?

JOANNA
                Yes. Can you hear me?

TROY
Yes, now I can. But these old devices
just don't work the way the new ones did.

JOANNA
I still expect to see you in a hologram
or at least on a screen. I guess those days
are over, but I'm not yet used to it.

TROY
At least these phones still work.
It seems so many things are breaking down.
I don't know how much longer this
connection will hold out.
Before we get cut off, I want to ask:
What else is happ'ning there
with the investigators?
I can imagine it is trying on the souls
of all the people living there
in our community.

JOANNA
They had some questions about children's safety
and health, and lower-school curriculum.
But otherwise, we don't know what they think.
In any case it's good that these inspectors
experience some human contact with
the life and work of this community.

TROY
It seems like such a shame to close the Hall.
But I suspect that that will be the least of it.

(*beat*)

JOANNA
Are you still there?

        TROY
            Yes, I'm still here. Joanna,
I want to tell you something. – –
I'm visiting a church here. I am going
to meet with someone there this morning.

JOANNA
A church? What do you mean, a church?

TROY
It's called "The Bridge of Christ".
Their spokesman was on all the news last year.
He mostly just got ridiculed.

JOANNA
I know about that church.
Other churches have
embraced the legal guidelines.
That church refuses to comply.

TROY
Yes. That's the one. I wanted to find out
what has become of it.
So I went to their service yesterday.

JOANNA
And what did you experience?

TROY
                    I felt
sheer peacefulness, and sensed a sacred presence.
I liked the way they spoke of Jesus Christ.

JOANNA
Oh Troy, religious faith is something of the past.
Our human consciousness has long evolved
beyond that stage. And that church is especially
archaic, rigid and inflexible,
grasping at scripture without knowledge.
But Benedictus often spoke about
this kind of pseudo-Christianity.
Instead of seeking the true Cosmic Christ,
they seek, mistakenly, a group-soul
or they see Jesus only as a man.

TROY
You know, I've never really understood
that disconnection.

JOANNA
I'm losing you again.

TROY
                    I am with you.

JOANNA
                    Be careful.
These people may seem very nice and good.
But they will judge you harshly and condemn you
if you do not believe what *they* believe
or if they find out that your way of life
is not in harmony with theirs.

(*Slight beat.*)

TROY
Joanna, may I ask you:
Are you planning to accept that new position?

JOANNA
I have accepted it already. Yes.

TROY
My heart sinks when you tell me that.
And yet there lives in me the hope
that love will show itself in many forms.

JOANNA
It's always been your nature to
unite your soul in love
with all the substance that life brings to you.

TROY
I hope to see you soon, when you are here.
Goodbye.

JOANNA
Goodbye, dear brother.

(*Beat. Barbara enters.*)

BARBARA
Joanna it's so good to see you here again.
Congratulations on
your new position in the government.
Your book must be regarded as a bond
uniting spirit life with governance.
I hope that the authorities
will soon be able, through this book,
to learn how solid is the base
of all our ways of working.
And that our principles for
the earth and for humanity
can truly coincide with world goals.

JOANNA
Oh, thank you, Bobby.
I hope that I've succeeded in
describing Benedictus' spirit science,
and work his students have derived from it,
in modern scientific terms
that world government authorities
and ordinary people of our time
can understand.
And this could make them willing to accept –
and even further implement and spread –
the ways of child development,
of education, and of farming, that
Stella Sophia developed with us here
in this community.
I'm glad that I could be here

to honor and remember Miss Sophia
and help with the inspections.
I'm sorry that we had to leave the Hall.
But how's all this affecting *you*?

BARBARA
I patiently await whatever comes.
Investigators finished at the school.
Robert has given them the information
that they requested. And today
they're looking at the dairy and the farm.
A few of them observed us as we milked
the cows this morning. And of course
they were surprised our cows have horns.
I talked with them about the preparations,
of burying the cow horns
filled with good manure,
and how we stir and spray
the substance we prepare from it.
They hadn't read your book yet, but
by being here among us, I know that
they experience within their heart
the spirit beings guiding what we do.
Even in those with souls still closed and stiff,
the good has been implanted
and will work on in them in future lives.
The time will come when they will hear
the voice of truth, and all these wild obscure
conceptions will appear to them quite normal.
For now they have a job to do.

JOANNA
I hope that I can speak with them myself.

BARBARA
Your new position is significant.
I wonder if you'd tell me more about it.
I like to grasp such things as clearly as I can.

JOANNA
Because my book has been so popular,
and it contains ideas they can embrace, the
United Union's offered me – and I've
accepted – a position as advisor to
the Cultural and Agricultural
Authorities.
I will be able to contribute to
the forming of environmental policies
and agricult'ral regulations,
as well as those for education.
This is an opportunity to bring
our spirit science into work where only
material science has held sway in life.

BARBARA
And tell me once again, so I can grasp,
how our new world government,
which we have long been hoping for,
will actually affect the lives of *farmers*
and the nutrition people get from food.

JOANNA
I haven't yet begun my work with them,
but leaders have made clear:
our freedom and our choice will be upheld.
Farming will not be so industrialized.
The long-established corporate food regime,
with its destructive impact on the earth, is
being dismantled by the world leaders.
The right of peoples to define
their food and farming methods for themselves
is almost guaranteed – as well as rights
to healthy, culturally appropriate food
produced through ecologic practices.
In setting policies for food,
the world Authority is putting those
who farm, produce, distribute and consume
(rather than demands of corporations
and economic markets) at the heart.

New policies include – and will defend –
the interests of the coming generations
by globally revitalizing rural areas
and equitably redistributing
the farmland and the water
and giving farmers the control of seeds.

BARBARA
And will our spirit science, through your book,
become well known as time goes on? And could
our farm and dairy here be an example?

JOANNA
I think that that may well be possible.
The Agricultural Authority
will offer guidelines
that will allow productive small-scale farms to
provide consumers locally grown food
and to determine their own ways of farming.
And we will give priority to local
and regional economies and markets,
now that the national economies
have been subsumed by world unity.
This will empower family farms
and farms that poorer farmers manage
so the environment, society
and economics can sustain them.

BARBARA
The fount of spirit knowledge and the work
that flows from it into our daily life,
which until now were kept and nurtured in
our close community, will through your work
with world authority be opened up
to all humanity. I see in you
the one who will unite our spirit research
with government authority –
who brings to modern politics
the knowledge of the spirit.

(*Robert Finn rushes in, interrupting.*)

ROBERT
Oh, Bobby! The investigators are
confiscating the equipment from the dairy.
They've shut us out and locked it down,
put chains on all the doors.
They poured out all the milk into the drain.
The yogurt and your cheeses are destroyed.

(*Beat. Blackout.*)

(*End of scene.*)

4) Between Two Worlds

(*The office of The Bridge of Christ, and the home of Michael Capstone and Meaghan Gerald. Meaghan is on the phone. Michael is taking off his coat. Later, the Other Philia appears.*)

MEAGHAN
Yes, that is right. It seems we are permitted
to hold our services and ritual
as long as we don't advertise. . . . .
Well, yes, it is. I do agree with you, George.
Yes, it's a limit on free speech. . . . .
They now consider it offensive speech;
It could offend those who have other faiths
 . . . yes . . . Yes. I know. Yes,
of course we will continue to resist this.
I don't. . . . Not yet, but it is possible.
We will. Of course, you're free to do as you
may choose, but you could be arrested and
it may have consequences for the church . . .
Yes. Michael's taking that responsibility.
Yes, thank you, George. I'll let him know. Good-bye.
(*She hangs up*)
Good morning, Michael. Ray can hold the service
with Blythe and me tomorrow morning so
you can go meet with the authorities.
Now George would like to go with you, of course.

CAPSTONE
I'll phone him. But it's best I go alone.

MEAGHAN
Yes, I agree. – –

CAPSTONE
We have a consultation still this morning?

MEAGHAN
That young man at the service yesterday.
The visitor I spoke to afterward.
He ought to be here shortly. (*Pause.*)
I wonder how you slept.
You cried out in the middle of the night –
again.

CAPSTONE
You heard me?

MEAGHAN
Yes. My door was open.

CAPSTONE
I had that dream again about a burning temple.
But this time I was trapped inside it
trying to save it and put out the flames.
But its round domes are all engulfed in smoke,
colorful tongues of fire, devouring
carved pillars that collapse and crash around me
until I am consumed in fire and smoke
and feel I've failed at some momentous task.
And I keep thinking of that passage in the Gospel:
"Destroy this temple, I will build it up."

MEAGHAN
This has been going on for weeks now.

CAPSTONE
But Meaghan, what do you suppose it means?

MEAGHAN
It seems to me that God is giving you
a picture of what's happ'ning to our church,
and to your work. You're toiling desperately
to save a burning edifice.

CAPSTONE
Perhaps it also is an image of
these urges that I feel, unspeakable
burning desires coming up again,
consuming me.
I celebrate our rituals, give my sermons;
I care for our parishioners, defend
our church from threats by world government.
But I don't know how I can still continue.
Why do I feel this urging of the body?
I know it's wrong.
I thought I had outgrown it long ago.
The struggle is depleting me;
I feel divided from myself
and sense that something has to change.
And so this dream of mine seems like a sign.

MEAGHAN
Oh, Michael, I'm distressed that you are haunted
by such tormenting pain within your soul.
It seems to me it is a craving
that is not yet transformed through love,
a shadow of yourself estranged from you,
which tears from you a sense of joy in life.
But I won't form a judgement of
temptations I have not experienced,
for you know well that sensual desires
have never troubled me that way.
I feel myself within God's loving forces,
which flame through me, empowering my soul;
I see the life of all humanity
as sparks across the surface of the earth.
I feel myself at one with God's eternal life
for which I know you strive unceasingly,
and which appears to us through Jesus Christ
as revelation of His being in us.
There was a time when you felt just the same.

Or so it seemed. Distractions of the flesh,
romantic interests, seemed to both of us a
needless diversion from God's work.
And so we married.

CAPSTONE
            Yes. That's why we married.
We joked of how you were my guardian
to keep the ladies at a prudent distance.

MEAGHAN
Yes, many women lovingly pursued you.

CAPSTONE
And many loving men pursued you, too.

MEAGHAN
And so you did the same for me. We married
to serve the Lord with certainty
and to protect and guard us each from such
entanglements, so that we could devote
ourselves with all our strength to do the work
that God was calling us to do for Him.

CAPSTONE
Yes. In our early days of partnership,
it seemed to me that the unnatural urges
that I saw rising from my depths of soul
should be defied, subdued or disregarded.
But now these feelings cannot be ignored.
I am afflicted by a passion that
opposes heaven's laws, and I must feel
what is not founded purely in God's kingdom.
Hot forces rising to my heart have violated
the stern decree of nature's ancient laws.
I should not, in my soul, direct toward men
thoughts that can open unfamiliar realms.
And yet I feel what I should never feel.
My disobedience is delivering
my life to demons in a realm of darkness.

My soul's afflicted by forbidden passion
within a region alien to God;
and what I thus experience is growing
to a consuming fire in my soul
and working further to destroy our church.

MEAGHAN
In this dark moment, my dear Michael, I
can see your soul is in deep peril.
I see you suff'ring and I know that you
must find your way through darkness to the light.

(*The Other Philia appears.*)

And yet I cannot help you in this quest
that seems so foreign to my soul.
Only the Lord, in whom we put our trust,
can help you find your way among these demons.

THE OTHER PHILIA
The One who has Risen
eternally offers
the bread of His body,
the wine of His blood,
for those who are bound
to the measures of earth.
But eyes are weighed down,
and an indolent heart
becomes pale and profaned
and as rigid as ice.
And lips sealed tight
are withholding the breath
that is cold and indifferent.
For the table forsaken
is always replenished,
but nothing is tasted
by those who abstain.

(*Another phone call, as the Other Philia disappears.*)

MEAGHAN
Oh. That may be our visitor who's coming. (*Answering phone*)
The Bridge of Christ; It's Meaghan Gerald speaking. . . .
Yes, it is. . . . Yes, it was. . . . Yes, he is. . . .
Yes, I'm his colleague. . . Yes, I am . . . .
Indeed, it's on his calendar.
Tomorrow. . . . . Ye-e-es . . . Yes, I've got it.
Yes, he'll be there. Good-bye.
(*To Capstone*) The Cultural Authority.
About your hearing in the morning.

CAPSTONE
I guess I'll have to do the best I can.
This is the consequence of speaking out.

MEAGHAN
I know it's not our way to be so public.
But under such distressing circumstances,
it did seem necessary. Someone had
to speak against the power of this Regime.
So now they are investigating us.

CAPSTONE
Ah, yes. We had our moment of brief fame.
Now the news media will not come near us.

MEAGHAN
Another safety officer came yesterday.
And we received a notice that
the audit of our taxes was inadequate.

(*The sound of a door buzz.*)

Oh. Here's our visitor. (*Phone rings.*)
Buzzer's not working. Could you get the door?

(*Capstone goes to the door and opens it.*)

MEAGHAN
(*Answering phone*)
The Bridge of Christ; it's Meaghan Gerald speaking.

(*Troy enters. Moment. Michael Capstone and Troy look at each other and seem to recognize each other.*)

TROY
Hello. My name is Mario,
but people call me Troy.

MEAGHAN
Yes, Blythe, we still intend to light the candles. –
– – – Yes, yes I know,
but they are part of our ritual
and we'll keep lighting them until
the fire authorities prevent it.
– – Thanks. See you then.

(*to CAPSTONE*) So sorry.
(*to Troy*) Please forgive the phone distraction.

TROY
I'm Troy Fels. We spoke on Sunday here.

MEAGHAN
Yes. Welcome. It is good to see you here again.
What brings you here?

TROY
An inner calling, I suppose.

MEAGHAN
Yes, people sometimes feel a calling to
our ritual and practices. Some,
through desperate situations and addictions,
have had direct experience of Christ.

TROY
I had seen Mr. Capstone on the news
last year when this church got so much attention.
His observations really moved me, so
I thought I'd try to meet him here in person.

MEAGHAN
I'll leave you two alone. (*She exits.*)
(*Beat.*)

TROY
I liked your sermon that you gave on Sunday.

CAPSTONE
I . . .

TROY
... felt like ... you were speaking right ... to me.

CAPSTONE
I guess I was ... in a way.
It wasn't what I'd planned. ... But when I saw
you sitting there – I somehow knew
I had to speak ... about true freedom.

TROY
It touched me very deeply –
this question of our inner and
our outer freedom . . . and the Christ.

CAPSTONE
It is through Jesus Christ that we attain
true Freedom.

TROY
      Yes.

CAPSTONE
      Now, won't you please, sit down.

TROY
I understand your church defies the statutes.

(*Capstone hesitates, then nods cautiously.*)

Forgive me. Let me start again.
You see, I come from a community
that's being stifled by United Union rules.
I thought that you might somehow help us,
or I might learn from your experience.

CAPSTONE
Is your community a Christian one?

TROY
Well, yes, it really is. Although sometimes
I think that people hide that. Or they tell me
we have to see the Cosmic Christ, not only
"the simple man of Nazareth" — but I
am not so sure that they are separate.

CAPSTONE
Since God and man became one . . .

TROY
                              . . . and still are.
One.

CAPSTONE
        Yes. In Jesus Christ.

TROY
                        Yes, surely that
is what they mean.
I know there was a time when darkness ruled
in human souls on earth, when all connection
with heaven and the angels had been lost.
And I know too that only once in time
there was a turning.

The light of spirit poured into our souls
when Christ lived as a man on earth.
And knowledge of this lives within the hearts
of those who form community in Him.

CAPSTONE
I'd like to learn more. Are there books?

TROY
Yes. It's still possible to order them
from the archives in Europe.

CAPSTONE
                Have you been to Europe?
I mean what still remains of it.

TROY
Yes, I've been living there for years.
Consulting, bringing spiritual ideas
and practices to psychiatric nursing care.

CAPSTONE
I'm sure that you do untold good
with your warm heart.

TROY
Sometimes I feel the weakness of my will,
as if I cannot live much longer.
The ever-growing regulations
and documenting, far beyond
what's necessary for good care,
exhaust my soul and life force, but
I often gain fresh strength
from the abundance flowing from
the fountain of the spirit. – –

CAPSTONE
– – I feel somehow I know you, . . .

TROY
Yes. . . . Me too.

(*speaking together*)

CAPSTONE	TROY
that there's	I see something. . .

CAPSTONE
Sorry.

TROY
No, go ahead.

CAPSTONE
that there's some reason that the Lord
has led you here.

TROY
                    Yes.

CAPSTONE
                    Yes. – –
What do you see? – – –

                    (*End of scene*)
                    (*End of Act I*)

Act Two

5) Dead Canary

*(A large room in the school of the Sophia Community. Joanna, then
Marcus; later Robert, Barbara, four denizens of the Sophia
Community, including Lucy, otherwise manifest as Lucifer but
appearing here in her earthly form. Ahriman as spirit only. Celia and
Stratham. It is to be imagined, later in the scene, that many other
people are present, in the direction of the audience.)*

(Joanna enters, speaking on her phone.)

JOANNA
Yes, locks and chains . . a dairy ... yes. That's it,
Ms. Harris. That's the situation. Yes. ...
I've spoken to the Agricultural
Authority already, but since I
am new there, I just thought that I would speak
to you as well. ... I would appreciate
anything you can do to set this right. ...
Yes. ... Thank you. I'll be waiting for a call, then.
*(She shuts her phone and looks around the empty space. She goes to
the refreshment table and pours herself a cup of coffee. Marcus
enters.)*

MARCUS
Joanna, it's so good to see you after all these years.
And I am pleased to find you so engaged
in your important work,
uniting spirit purposes
with the reality of the new world regime.
I overheard your last words on the phone.
So do you think there's something you can do
about the milk?

JOANNA
I'm puzzled that investigators thought
they had to close the dairy. They insist

that it's a safety issue and they have
a mandate from the world court.
I'm confident that we can work it out.
I've called the Agricultural Authority
as well as Health and Safety and
a colleague who I think can help.
Someone will call me soon.   –
Are people coming in here for the story?

MARCUS
Not yet. They're gathering in the barn,
shocked and upset about the dairy, but
rousing their strength and singing to the cows.

JOANNA
That's beautiful. I'm sure they need it now.
We used to sing to them on Christmas eve
with Miss Sophia. – Your speech just now . . . .
it was as if she spoke through you.
And then my mother saw and heard her . . .
   – – –
I'm sorry Troy couldn't stay to see you.

MARCUS
Although I feel my soul is incomplete
without his warmth,
he knows he has my blessing and my love,
wherever he may stumble.
From my soul depths rose up an om'nous warning
I was unable to deny or silence –
a thought that touched my beings deepest core,
although it seemed to me like blasphemy:
Within my heart I felt quite clearly
that Troy and I must go our separate ways;
we must not hold our love unto ourselves,
but find it in the world each on his own.
I must remember love is wisdom's sister
and let him go. If he returns,
the world will be encompassed by our love.

JOANNA
But still, I'm sorry that he cannot be here
to comfort you and honor Miss Sophia.

MARCUS
Yes. Her death has left me numb.
I feel that something of myself has died.

JOANNA
Her death's a blow for all of us,
but you were very close to her. –
It seemed as if she'd live forever.
She was timeless.

MARCUS
          Yes. – –

JOANNA
          – We seem
to have a moment's peace now to ourselves.
And this may be our only chance to talk.

MARCUS
Yes. That is why I sought you out just now.
What did you want to speak to me about?

JOANNA
We've known each other all our lives, although
we haven't seen each other since our youth.
And now there is a riddle plaguing me,
which also concerns you.
I'm grateful that the powers of destiny
guided my parents to this school
and that we met here. – –
Do you remember Miss Sophia speaking
about her foster mother, who
was very close to Benedictus?

MARCUS

                    Yes.

JOANNA
Ever since Miss Sophia told us of her,
I've made it my life goal to be like her.
In many situations, I will ask,
what would Maria do?
Of course I've read what you have sent me,
out of the archives, about her.
I'm always striving to develop
her strength of spirit and
her clarity and selfless love.

MARCUS
You know, they say she also had her faults.

JOANNA
Yes. After Benedictus died. I know.
I understand those times were difficult.
I hope that I can learn from them as well.
There's more I want to say: Remember when
Stella Sophia taught us Norse
Mythology and culture in Fourth Grade?
We both had the idea we knew each other then.

MARCUS
Yes, I remember, now you mention it.

JOANNA
You were a Druid Christian missionary
who came into my tribe
and you converted me.
We pictured Miss Sophia there as well.

MARCUS
(*Laughing*) Yes, I remember now.
We saw her as a stubborn heathen,
bitterly faithful to the Nordic gods and

resisting all my teaching of the Christ.
I haven't thought of that in years.

JOANNA
I have. It's somehow always stayed with me.
And then in high school, I had such a crush on you.
And I remember you and Troy
always debating, arguing about
the origin and the philosophy
behind our school. I knew then, destiny
had wisely brought you near each other.

MARCUS
Ah yes, you knew that before I did.

JOANNA
You were such complementary opposites –
yes, even then, contrasting, balancing
each other. *Your* clear light and *his* deep warmth.
Your uprightness and his wide breadth
of interest and enthusiasm.
I knew your love for me was noble, but
I had to recognize and to accept
that you would never want to marry me.
And yet I sensed my paths of life
were closely linked to yours.
I've always counted you my closest friend.
For it's become as clear to me as truth itself:
some thorny road of destiny has joined us.
You live within my thinking, even from
so far away, across the global oceans.
And as I've dedicated my whole life
to academic work and active thinking,
uniting spiritual science with
contemporary thought, you've guided me
in studying the work of Benedictus
and of Thomasius, his noted pupil.
Then, when my husband died, I had the vivid,
and palpable experience of fulfillment.

Caring for him through all his illnesses
resolved some karmic debt and I felt free.
It also then became still clearer to me,
that on my spirit path it is with you
I have the closest bond.
And so I feel I have to tell you that –
as I take on this role in world government
and seek to bring our spirit science
more openly into world destiny –
a voice, deep within my soul,
cries out repeatedly
"If you would not do harm, you must
know *who* you are in world destiny,
which leads you onward to your goal."
(*beat*)
I have some inkling who I was
in previous lives and why
I have the tasks I have in this one.
I asked my brother what he saw.
And Troy, with his vision, could
confirm my thoughts.
You've shown to me the high truth that
a veil of illusion covers the surface of our life.
And yet I need to have clear knowledge,
if I'm to bear my destiny.
And so I feel I have to ask you now:
Do you know who you were in
in any of your previous lives on earth?

MARCUS
Oh, dear Joanna, no, I don't know who I was.
I understand your curiosity. But
I think it's better not to speculate
about such things.
Once Benedictus taught how spirit
can fill the soul with light, and can
unite itself in inward warmth
with everything that in the depths of life
spins human destiny.

And yet I know that my own thinking
can only weave dim shadows
of the real sources of our being.
I cannot read the Book of Life,
the Cosmic Record, and
I don't think we had the capacity
to read it when we were in high school.
To try to guess about past lives
can only lead into illusion.
Benedictus gave us certain exercises
to help us to develop the capacities
to see such things. And any other way
is dangerous and bound to lead to error.
I know that Troy has visions and believes
that he can see past lives of people back
to the beginning of the earth.
We've talked about it many times.
I never asked him what he sees of mine.
You know how much we love each other.
But he is rarely able
to ground his knowledge and experience
in statements Benedictus really made
and what he wrote.
And now it seems that he
is turning to religion.
He doesn't seem to understand
that churches now
have no real knowledge of the Christ.
He'll have to learn that for himself.
Joanna, do your inner work,
as Benedictus has presented it.
And study what he actually wrote.
Your book and work will be a service to
humanity. But do not lose yourself
or squander your attention
in speculating about other lives.
I know that that is not what you
wanted to hear, and it grieves me.

(Joanna sits, absorbing this in silence. Robert Finn enters, catching Marcus's last words.)

ROBERT
Oh, Mr. Lilly, please don't grieve.
My wife wants me to tell you,
all will be well: The times are changing.
Oh, and I'm sorry about Miss Sophia's ashes:
  – I know you wanted
to take them to the Temple Monument.
But – well – Troy took them. –

MARCUS
Oh. To ... the ...

ROBERT
Stella Sophia always said she wanted
to plant something in the Midwest.
Her teacher, Benedictus, told her that
a bridge to spirit work should spring up in
the "heartland" of America.

(Marcus is silent. Tears well up. Denizens of the Sophia Community enter, among them Lucy. Then Celia and Simon Stratham, who remain quietly observing at the back.)

FIRST DENIZEN
It seems to me that we the people *are*
the government. With this world unity,
which I feel could be truly Micha'elic
with leaders who're good-hearted and like-minded,
humanity itself can now create a better world.

SECOND DENIZEN
The corporate and industrial approaches
to education, agriculture and
to social care did not enable people
to choose to live, free individuals
in a community, as we have done
here vibrantly for decades.

THIRD DENIZEN
But now we'll have to drink the standard milk
that's mass produced by
the global Agricultural Authority.
Or else we'll go without.
It isn't good what's in that standard milk.

(*Barbara Finn enters.*)

And our milk isn't yet protected or
permitted by the regulations.

ROBERT
                    Bobby.

(*Everyone looks to her.*)

What's happened now? What did they say to you?

BARBARA
They're charging me with criminal offense:
distributing unpasteurised – raw – milk.
But I am confident our rights and freedoms
will be protected in the end.
If we approach this rightly, we'll find justice.
If only they would sit and talk with us,
I could explain to them just how our milk is safe.
They could have tested our raw milk
before destroying it. They could have seen
the health of all of us who drink it.
But they will learn – I have no doubt of it.
Humanity evolves through times of change.
Things alter and become their opposite.
I follow spirit guidance either way.
Now if the children had been taken from
their parents, then I willingly would risk my life:
go on a hunger strike or beat down doors.

CELIA
Oh, Barbara! I feel I have to tell you:
I see a budding light, a child hovering around you,
seeking to come into the world with special tasks.
It's chosen you. If you are carrying
a child, you mustn't risk your life in protest.

ROBERT (*putting his arm around her*)
She really is most happy when
she's tending to the garden and the cows.
The nature beings speak to her.
And when she was a little girl
they were her dearest playmates.
Elves and sprites and gnomes,
the dryads, nyads, sylphs and undines.
And they have never left her.
In quiet moods of inner stillness,
they, even now, reveal to her
what's needed in the garden or in life.

BARBARA
A spirit guidance also speaks within my heart.
I follow it obediently,
whether it leads me into solitude
or into turmoil of the agitated crowd.
But if a child comes to us,
we will provide a peaceful home.

ROBERT
Well, I don't get much peace at school. A teacher's
required to do much more administration
these days: forms, tests and documents to write.
So I have less and less time with the children.

FIRST DENIZEN
Yet, documenting what we do is good
and necessary in the modern world.
Everyone has to do it. Why should we
be any different? And inspections help
assure the quality of work as well as safety
and good health for all.

SECOND DENIZEN
We can be grateful the investigators
have now decided, after all,
not to pursue the charges of neglect
or take the children from their parents.

THIRD DENIZEN
The only so-called crime was that
the children hadn't been
injected with required medications.
And that they played outdoors
without the supervision of adults,
riding their bicycles without a helmet,
climbing in trees. Where else but here
are children still allowed to have a childhood?

SECOND DENIZEN
And what about our festivals, the plays
that classes in our school produce each year,
concerts and therapeutic work,
the glorious choir of bells,
rung by our friends with special skills and needs?
These things don't happen elsewhere anymore.

THIRD DENIZEN
And when will we again stand by the river,
watching a schoolboy launch a boat he's made
with his own hands? And celebrate the similar
unique accomplishments of all his classmates?
Such simple beauty and capacities
are all but lost outside this settlement.
And even here they're threatened more and more.

FOURTH DENIZEN
Yes, many people say our movement's died.
And that the work and impulses
of Stella Sophia's teacher Benedictus
just haven't taken hold, that we have failed
to work together, deepening

our knowledge of the spirit, nurturing
our souls and one another, and
applying spiritual knowledge practically
to the conditions of our modern life.

AHRIMAN (*appearing only to the audience*)
Ah, yes. Their work has failed. They will forget
what long ago they had begun. Unique,
creative, human beings will vanish from the earth.
Their children will be coldly taken from them
and locked indoors, forgetting how to play.
Their Festivals, by law, will be forbidden.
Their milk and honey will be drained and spoiled.
Drowned out by discord and cacophony,
their music and their laughter will fall silent.
Art will cease. Apocalypse approaches.
(*He disappears.*)

SECOND DENIZEN
Yet many have devoted all their will to
preserve and re-enliven spirit science,
ever since Benedictus' death, and
division, strife and turmoil
threatened his spiritual work on earth.
And our community right here
across the ocean,
until now, has thrived.

LUCY
You have all misinterpreted the situation
if you believe that any outward power
can harm the spiritual work
of those who gather round me here.
For sorrows and anxieties
cannot creep into souls who trust
in blissful light and joy of spirit,
which bring you freedom from such earthly cares.
(*She exits.*)

BARBARA
We must remember that true impulses,
planted like seeds in good and fertile soil –
if only we continue tending them –
will yield fruit, when time has been fulfilled.
Our aspirations will work on,
so long as we are guided by the spirit.
(*to Marcus Lilly*)
But now I must express to you
how much my heart rejoices
to welcome for the first time here among us
a man we've heard so much about.
We hope to see you now more often here.

MARCUS
Joanna and I went to school together here,
when I came here from Europe as a youth.
But that was well before your time.

ROBERT
(*Greeting Stratham*)
Joanna's father, Simon Stratham,
is also with us here today.
The field of psychology
has always seemed quite strange to me,
all full of abstract notions and typologies.
But I was glad when I found out about
Stratham's new work. It's real and doable.
I've followed the development of his
techniques. They're reaching many many people,
who can apply them in their daily life.

STRATHAM
It is a small but genuine antidote to
many unhealthy forces in our modern life.
But, Robert, won't you please continue
the Tale of Miss Sophia's life.

(*The Denizens begin to find seats in the audience or on either side downstage, Celia, Simon, Marcus and Barbara as well, waiting for Robert to continue his story.*)

FOURTH DENIZEN
Yes. You were just beginning when
we had to leave the Hall.

JOANNA
I am expecting an important call
about the milk. So please excuse me. Sorry
I'll have to miss the rest of Robert's story.
But anyway, I need some time alone.
(*She exits.*)

BARBARA
These stories Robert tells
are true food for the soul,
full of images that nourish us
even beyond our death.
They hold a living seed of spirit science,
the modern path of knowledge.
And if you listen carefully,
you'll find he tells a story
in many different ways.

SECOND DENIZEN
Hearing a story will do us some good.

ROBERT
Does anyone remember where we were?

MARCUS
She was a child on Maria's doorstep.

ROBERT
Ah yes.
(*He gathers himself a brief moment, then speaks to the audience*)
The wise and radiant woman had
no children and no husband,

and so it seemed that she was destined
to care for and to raise this child
who had appeared upon her doorstep.
And so she did.
With motherly devotion and with love,
with skill and wisdom from her teacher
she cared for and she guided this young child,
a little girl, through her early life.
And when the child needed greater wisdom,
the woman's teacher came to visit.
The child sat upon his fatherly lap,
and he would guide her with stories
and with rhymes and verses.
The child lived happily, surrounded by
the love and warmth of her new foster mother.
But one day, a seeress from
the circle of her foster mother's friends
was visiting at the woman's house.
The little child saw the seeress' eyes
begin to glow with an unearthly light.
The seeress spoke in a strange voice
of the future appearance of the Christ.
Frightened, the child ran
into her foster mother's arms.
For some time after that,
the child would not speak,
and ate but little.
Indeed it seemed that she had died –
although she was quite healthy physically.
Her soul was dark.
In great distress,
the child's foster mother sought
the help of her great teacher.
Through him she came to know,
her foster child was tied to her from
a long past life on earth,
and now was seeking wisdom she
had long ago rejected and attacked.
The teacher told the child a story,

and this is how it went:
      'A beautiful Princess, Lily,
lived in a palace with a beautiful garden.
But she was enchanted by a curse.
For every living thing she touched would die,
but anyone who met the power of her eyes
would live – devoid of spirit.
She had a pet canary, who would sing
a lovely melody and sit upon
the Lily's harp, as she too sang.
So long as the pet canary never touched
the Lily, all was well.
      'One day a hawk flew overhead
and in a fright the pet canary
flew to the Lily's breast for comfort,
but upon touching her, fell dead
onto the ground at her feet.
Many friends and creatures came
to try to help and comfort
the Lily as she stood there weeping
in her garden. With their help
and many wondrous deeds of transformation and
of love, the power of the Lily's touch reversed,
and the canary fluttered overhead,
returned to life.'
And when the foster child had heard this story,
all was well. She gradually returned
her foster mother's love
and grew and thrived within her care.
Even her mother's circle
of friends grew dear to her.
And as these friends all worked and played together,
they built a sacred Temple filled with strange
and wondrous forms and colors.
Then one dark night the child, now grown, stood
among the crowd of helpless people,
watching the colors and shapes go up in flames.
And the beloved Temple burned
to the ground.

There was a pear tree, growing near the Temple,
and it was scorched within the fire and
everyone thought the tree had died.
But the following spring,
leaves sprouted on its branches
and the tree lived.
When the circle of friends had lived their lives
and done their deeds and died,
the child now grown to womanhood, took
a living twig from the Temple's tree
and carried it far away across the sea
and planted it. It grew and bore much fruit.
Children climb it and the pears are sweet.
And that is the pear tree here outside our school.
(*Sighs, smiles, quiet or silent applause.*)

FOURTH DENIZEN
Beautiful. Thank you.

STRATHAM
(*Shaking his hand warmly*)
Yes. Thank you, Robert. You have given us
a beautiful picture of our dear Stella Sophia's life.
And we have all been nourished by the fruit
borne of the tree that she has planted here.

FIRST DENIZEN
Yes, it's a perfect metaphor.
But is it also true? Is our pear tree really from
the one outside the temple monument?

ROBERT
Yes. Miss Sophia told me that herself.

SECOND DENIZEN
It is quite possible to grow a tree,
just starting from a cutting, isn't it?

FOURTH DENIZEN
Yes, of course. I've done it many times.
Since Miss Sophia taught me in First Grade.

THIRD DENIZEN
She taught us many things. She will be missed.

STRATHAM
She was my teacher too.
In lower grades. We thought she was
an old woman even then.
To us she was. Old and wise.

ROBERT
And how old *was* she when she died?

STRATHAM
More than a hundred, certainly.
But no one knows for sure.
Maybe a hundred twenty.
Incredible I know,
yet there has always been
something quite mythical about her being.

BARBARA
You know, it seemed as if she'd live for centuries.
Since I was just a little girl,
I've had ability at certain moments
to see, by grace, a person's life force.
In her, this force appeared to me unending.
It seemed to come from long past ages and
continue undiminished.
And so she lived a long, long life
and served the suff'ring world
for many, many decades.

(*Denizens, Marcus, Barbara and Celia exit, as Robert and Stratham
speak more intimately.*)

ROBERT
(*to Stratham*)
I can imagine *your* work also as
a tree that's growing from a twig
transplanted from a former work on earth –
from Benedictus and his pupils.
It seems to me that, at a time
when human bodies are so hardened,
your new techniques were given by the gods to
allow humanity to still transform
ourselves, within these hardened bodies,
through our own free will.

STRATHAM
Yes, anyone can learn and then apply
these new techniques to all aspects of life –
alone, with others, anywhere at all
and any time. I hope that they can be
a source of inner growth as well
as outer healing. –
It might have been a possibility
more than a century ago
through similar techniques,
for human forces of life to be
harnessed in an actual machine
or technical device for use at home.
But this potential has now been displaced
by various electronic gadgetry
on which the spirit of deceit,
holds his tight grasp – to either serve our will
or force us blindly to serve his.

ROBERT
I thank the gods that your work does not serve
that fierce sclerotic spirit of the darkness,
whom Benedictus made well known to us
as Ahriman. For your work uses forces
and knowledge from his realm to serve mankind's
becoming, granted by the plans of gods.

STRATHAM
If only I could be as sure as you
that my work only serves the will of gods.
This was my aim when I began. But now,
although my vision can still reach those realms
where inspiration flows into my soul,
my thinking heart and understanding are
obscured in darkness and I cannot see
the lasting consequences of my work.
And if I try to see, my vision dies.

ROBERT
Your vision dies? Your sweeping spirit vision,
which brought to light techniques for healing souls,
and guides your family and community?
You, Dr. Stratham, whose initiate gaze
can clearly see within the kingdom of
the Lord of Darkness? More than anyone,
you have been able to confront and to distinguish
what can be gained from that harsh spirit's realm
to bring clear knowledge and capacities
into our time. How can your vision die now?
Who can destroy your clear initiate gaze?

STRATHAM
Joanna flees with it to realms of darkness.
I must now follow her – and tread once more
into the realm where Ahriman is king.
His gloom is dampening my soul;
my fire dwindles, threatens to snuff out.
My thinking heart now struggles to persist;
Joanna smothers it in cosmic fog.
Where is my light? – Mere embers, I perceive
fierce darkness radiating round about me,
pouring confusing darkness into light,
my spirit day that once shone bright and clear.

(*During these last words, Celia re-enters.*)

CELIA
I feel that I must speak: Have courage Simon.
I see an angel standing over you,
a glorious messenger beckoning with wisdom,
announcing a great deed we must perform.
A temple waits in nearest spirit realms,
longing to be filled with active souls
and spirit work. And fierce, dark Ahriman,
with all his might, would like to crush this temple
and shroud the world in his eternal darkness.

(End of scene)

6) Joy on Spirit Wings

(Pleasant landscape. Michael Capstone and Troy Fels are walking together in peaceful conversation.)

CAPSTONE
When I'm with you, my worries disappear.
Now, tell me how you found your way
to work in psychiatric nursing.

TROY
I had this inner urge –
to work with people who'd been brought
by destiny to suffering and need.
And then, you know, I often found
it was their pain of soul that needed healing,
rather than only physical disease.

CAPSTONE
And even as a child you felt this urge?

TROY
My childhood was happy –
filled with abundant joyful life.
I thrived in school and in the festivals
of our community.
And when I could begin
to learn of spirit teachings,
then I could feel their warm and magic power
stream down into my hands and through my words.
I felt this power could bring strength and comfort
to those weighed down with sorrow
and to their pain-wracked hearts.
Although my parents had their own
spiritual experiences and tasks,
they've always stayed involved
with Miss Sophia's community.
And when I went to nursing school
and worked in sterile hospitals,

I found that ever and again
my inner source of strength
came not from my own will
in all its weakness,
but from the truth of words from spirit science,
which daily would create themselves anew
within me and would give me life.
And then my warmth of love joined forces with
the light of love that Marcus shone.
We were united once again in wholeness
for truly we're each other's other half.
But after many years, as more and more
I found the source of love within myself,
I found that what had flowed abundantly
between us and within our common work
was growing weaker and more feeble.
And it was this that led me
to seek out new horizons in the world,
to find out whether other hearts can feel
the spirit sources of the truth.
And that is what I'm finding here
in you and your community.
My own life forces blossom here again.
Fresh courage streams into my heart. . . .

CAPSTONE
I love the way you lift
our conversation into poetry.
If only I could speak like that,
in sermons, to our congregation.

TROY
The way you speak and pray is strange to me.
But if I inwardly transform your words,
and let them then resound out of my being,
they spread out, through my deeds and work,
over the world surrounding me,
and answer many riddles.

CAPSTONE
If what you say is true, then can you translate
for me what lives as deepest questions
within my heart, into your language? –
Questions about our times, of good and evil
of body, blood and truth that sets us free?
I sense that you could help me speak
with the great Mother . . . In the Book of Proverbs
she is called Wisdom. "Does not Wisdom call . . . ?"
She seems to me to be like the Madonna. And
through Meaghan I can often hear her voice.
That's what unites us, not the usual
attraction of a man and woman.
The Bible says, Her mouth will utter truth.
And She loves those who love Her,
and those who seek Her diligently, find Her.
"The Lord created me in the beginning,
first of his acts of old." And "he who finds me
finds life." – You seem to seek and find her.

TROY
You know, I think you see in me
a humble mirror image of our
Sophia community and all its friends.
I wish that Marcus could meet you,
he'd see the goodness of your thoughts and ways.
He still opposes what he thinks
that churches like yours stand for.
But he could translate for you
the revelations of our spirit teaching,
if only I could build a bridge
from you to him.
I sense that much depends on that.
It never will go well with us
and our community,
if we do not discover such a bridge.

CAPSTONE
If you say we must meet, then meet we will,
for you awaken in my manhood's breast

a childlike soul, naively true,
untouched by dogma and theology.
I sense a birth of knowledge bringing freedom.
The fruits that ripen from the springs of life,
are solving riddles and revealing secrets.

TROY
I feel I have to tell you that within
a little while, you will not see me here.

CAPSTONE
You told me that you cannot stay here long.

TROY
There is a place where green and jealous demons
defend their secrets in the cov'r of darkness.
If you will go there with me,
soaring on spirit wings, strengthened by warmth
of all the joy and pleasure we can share,
then riddles we are wrestling with can be unveiled
to human beings in the trembling light
and strength in us will grow to greatest heights.
Then all the beings of that realm will surely
become illumined by majestic beauty.

CAPSTONE
When you speak so poetically, I'd like to
accompany you into such a place.

TROY
Sometimes I feel inspired to speak like this.
I feel a fiery love within my heart
that wants to form itself in words
that rise out of the depths
from warmth of soul.
For many years
the clarity of Marcus' light of thought,
imbued with purest love,
would meet these words and give them meaning.

But then there came a time when that seemed lost.
His loving light no longer could illumine
in me my longing from the depths.
And so I seek to offer up my warmth
of words and healing deeds elsewhere,
as Marcus shines his light
into the world without my warmth.

CAPSTONE
Already I can see the days approach
when, changed, you'll find each other once again.
The man I see before me, walking here,
won't stay aloof from such a spirit light.
I know that you could not remain apart
from him for long – even if you wished.

(End of scene)

7) Devouring Thoughts

(Ahriman's realm. A dark gorge, black masses of rock, skeletons
everywhere, crystallized out of the mountain. No sky is visible.
Ahriman is seated on a rock, not visible at first; Astrid is also
somewhere on stage, not yet distinguishable in the darkness. Stratham;
then Trauta S. Harris and Joanna; later on Meaghan Gerald, Blythe
Truegood and Raymond Gumption; last of all Celia.)

STRATHAM
Again I have to step into this place.
Yet all the tools and wisdom I have gained here
will be creative in the world's becoming
only so long as spirit light upholds me.
Here comes the dreadful Father of this realm;
I know by how he radiates his strength
that he still feels unvanquished.

AHRIMAN
(to Stratham)   You have done
a bold deed in the course of human fate.

STRATHAM
And yet, unfortunately, I must admit
your powers have been active in my work.

AHRIMAN
Does good turn into bad because it stems
from my strength in this icy realm of truth?

STRATHAM
Whether it's good or bad, what I accomplish
through *you* is not worth anything to me.

AHRIMAN
Consider how you talk and note that you
have not removed the veil from your eyes,
which you may wear over there,
but which is here quite out of place.

Over there within the realm of earth,
reasons brewed up by knowledge seem to be
decisive. But over here it's power and will.
Here you stand spirit facing spirit.
Your way of talking over there
has to fall silent over here.
You point to this yourself whenever you
appear here. For you'd have to laugh
if you would talk to us with earthly reasons.
Nothing is refuted here;
here we swap realities. And
reality is what you want to gain
whenever you come visiting us here.
So name what you desire; and with our forces
you shall continue conquering on earth.

STRATHAM
Your words tell me that you
will yield powers to me this time too.

AHRIMAN
You seem to take yourself
to be especially strong this time.
But let us leave aside appearances;
What is it you're demanding here?

STRATHAM
The work I've done,
techniques I have discovered and developed
for healing soul and body and
for harmonizing human lives,
I wish to liberate from all your influence,
so that it only serves the good.

AHRIMAN
Surely you don't believe a deed you've done
can ever free itself from you. It will
remain bound up with you. It may appear
as if you have accomplished something good
and so can now work further good.

But I can see within your soul,
dark forces that you've still not mastered,
which therefore can be captured for my cause.
And then your work with all it's good intentions,
will fall to me. The truth will lead to error
and harden human souls you sought to heal.
And what is more, the part of your soul forces
that you would need to free your work from darkness,
I've taken as deposit for the insight
your daughter's borrowed from here for her work.

STRATHAM
Joanna – taken insight from you? – For
her book and her campaign for social change?
And you are holding my own soul force ransom!
I demand it back.

AHRIMAN
I cannot give it back. – Until Joanna,
through power of my greatest enemy,
awakens in herself the inner strength
to fully recognize the influence
that I have had on her, and until you
can think me as in truth I really am.
You cannot manage this for you are lamed.
But only then would I have to relinquish
what I have taken as a guarantee
against the generous loan I made to her,
for only then would she have paid it back.
And so her work remains my property.

STRATHAM
O forces of my soul, where shall I turn
to find the wellsprings I'm in need of here?
My soul's in anguish and uncertainty
whether a victory or destruction
will come to meet my firm resolve.

(Astrid's voice is now heard. She is hidden somewhere on stage, not yet visible.)

VOICE OF ASTRID
The budding powers of will
are fettered by
uncertain spirit sensing,
which paralyzes yearning.
Your feeling of yourself
is severed from devoted love;
my power of soul is forfeited
so that you cannot fathom
your own true being.

STRATHAM
Whenever I have stepped across this threshold,
I've hoped that victory would be decisive
over the beings for whom our earth existence
is worthless, and who only try to meddle
in human destiny on earth because
they want to capture it for alien goals.
How long will I still have to serve these powers?
(Astrid now becomes visible, she is in chains, covered in a dark veil.)

ASTRID
I'm banished here
from joyful sunlight,
from distant stars
and magic power of worlds,
from mighty spirit heights
and the ethereal azure heavens.
You cannot reach far-distant suns
as long as your own being is robbed of me.
Your heart has lost my power of soul,
its radiant beams;
and so the glowing warmth of knowledge
destroys itself in you.

STRATHAM
O spirits of the world's unfolding,
I've taken on the task to fight for you,
whose ways embody th' earth's true mission.
Only if my soul's unwavering,
can gods succeed
in vanquishing these enemies.
How can I free you, Astrid, from this darkness?

ASTRID
Within this realm of darkness I am bound
until the soul who lives now as your daughter
can recognize the one who holds me here.
As long as spirit sight is blind in her
and full awakened consciousness asleep
and powerless, unable to perceive
and know the Lord of Death in all his guises,
I will remain enslaved within this kingdom
where, hard'ning in rigidity, I die.
Preserver of my being – do not forsake me.

AHRIMAN
He will forsake you. For without your power,
he is too weak to rouse Joanna's soul
from slumber.   –   –

(*Astrid disappears again into the darkness.*)

There is a flaw in his soul depths as well:
a weakness in primeval fire forces.
In ancient temple rites, a word withheld
had left a breach that opened ever wider,
sundering him from his salvation's light.

STRATHAM
I'm well aware my soul is lamed.
But I will stand unwavering, steadfast
within your realm. I pity you in all
your pain and weep at what you have to do.
Although I see how cosmic deeds

are strengthened by your opposition –
for the hammer swinging in the dark
would never forge the iron
without the anvil's firm resistance –
yet I will join myself with many souls
and Celia, in harmony of spirit.
Though I have lost the power in my soul
to speak of you with radiant clarity,
I will remain awake while I am here.
Now show me what you know.

AHRIMAN
If I thought you would ever return to earth
rememb'ring what you've heard and seen while here,
I'd never speak to you like this.
But since I know whatever happens here
falls quickly out of human consciousness,
I'll speak to you. So watch. And you will see
what only here is known about my work.

(The soul of Trauta S. Harris now appears.)

This soul has long been faithful to my cause.
She's served me many times in many lives,
destroyed for me two temples and a castle.
And she once shook your faith and confidence
and caused your soul to badly doubt itself
by pointing out an error in your thinking.
Although that effort ultimately failed,
she served me well. And now serves even better.
I use her clever thinking to enforce
my plans to strengthen earth authority
that dampens souls, extinguishing the spirit.
She fancies she is a philosopher,
and has the scholarly degrees to prove it.

TRAUTA HARRIS
Philosophy can teach us that good sense
and understanding that develop of
their own accord can fathom worldly riddles.

And she who wants to find her way in life
must seize what profits her and gives her joy.

AHRIMAN
She's used her cleverness of thought to gain
her office and prestige in government.
She's useful to me there and does my bidding.
She thinks she thinks her*self*,
but all her thinking's only thoughts
that I implant in her while she's asleep.
And she has helped me to impose these thoughts
successfully upon her colleague here.
(*Joanna enters, blind, asleep, unaware of where she is. Trauta recedes
and exits.*)

STRATHAM
Joanna!

AHRIMAN
She only comes here as a sleeping soul,
knows nothing of my influence on her
and cannot understand what we are saying.
In her last life she blunted her own wit
against my mighty shadow. She knew me.
So I could not get at the man she was.
And with the soul who's now called Marcus Lilly
it was just the same,   –   –
until, through her, I gained my greatest victory
against that fellowship of Benedictus' pupils.
So there is always hope that I will conquer
those souls who may seem lost to me. –
And now that they've returned to earth again
in latter days, I've easily misled them,
by casting over their world view a fog,
which seems to them the light of clearest day.
Because this fog seems virtuous,
all sprinkled with their spiritual teachings,
they take it for the truth.

JOANNA
(*as in a trance*)
Equality in human life must be enforced.

AHRIMAN
She doesn't realize when awake that I've
inscribed this principle into her soul.

STRATHAM
But people *should* be equal in their rights,
before the laws that rule and govern men
and women in their dealings on the earth.

AHRIMAN
I will make all men equal in their *spirit* life
and so set up my kingdom on the earth.
And my success is now almost complete,
to spread into all spheres of people's lives
what rightly governs in their earthly laws,
within the realm of rights: They now believe
their *souls* are equal too, or that they should be.
Where gods ordain that other truths should guide,
the law of law – equality – will reign.

JOANNA (*again, as in a trance*)
The rule of men and women must make sure,
through centralized authority that all is good,
that everyone is safe and taken care of.

AHRIMAN
Karma must cease.
For I will stop the debts of destiny
from ever being balanced on the earth.
No one will be able or allowed
to take responsibility for risk
of life and limb by his or her own deeds.
All interactions will be mechanized
so everyone's entitled to be safe.
And this will then make everyone the same.

STRATHAM
In this dark, dreadful place one can observe
cold truths that can't be seen in other realms.
And yet what here can be perceived as truth
can cause destruction when applied on earth.

JOANNA (*as before*)
Men's actions always are destroying nature.
The earth would be much better off without them.

AHRIMAN
With help from faithful brother Lucifer,
this thought as well flows through her soul and work.

JOANNA
The greatest hope to save the earth is to
reduce effects humanity may have
and minimize the deeds of human beings,
so Nature can continue on its own.

AHRIMAN
Unconsciously, she's swallowed the idea
humanity's an accidental and
dispensable caprice of evolution.
And so her noble ideology
helps me to nullify the human thing.   (*Joanna exits.*)

STRATHAM
Then who can save the dying earth existence?

AHRIMAN
Only my greatest enemy of all,
who hides where human hearts will never seek.

STRATHAM
You always find delight in contradictions,
so I will seek the answer from myself.

(*Blythe Truegood, Raymond Gumption and Meaghan enter.*)

RAYMOND
This is the place within the spirit realm
that brings all thinking sternly to a standstill.

BLYTHE
Here, every seed must first succumb to death
before the life within it can return.

MEAGHAN
"Unless a grain of wheat
falls into the earth and dies,
it remains alone;
but if it dies, it bears much fruit."

RAYMOND
Just as the light can only see itself
with its own power of radiance, through reflection,
thinking can fathom its own nature by
casting us up on rocks of opposition,
causing grave doubts within the soul.
So here, a soul can learn to know itself in thinking.

MEAGHAN
I thank you that you've brought me to this place.
Now I will find my further way alone.

(*Blythe and Raymond exit.*)

STRATHAM
Who is this now? I've only rarely seen
another soul awake within this realm.

MEAGHAN
And who are you, you who have called me here?

STRATHAM
I called you here?

(*Celia appears*)

CELIA
I am compelled to enter this dark realm
to speak what from the worlds of gods
must be revealed lovingly to you.

AHRIMAN
It's getting very busy here.
For many eons I was here alone
and scarcely anyone came through
besides the throngs of sleeping souls at night
and those who lose their way in death.
But lately hardly any day goes by
without some searching soul come stumbling in.

CELIA
A shining light springs from your brow, dear Simon,
and shapes itself into a human form,
a solitary Jew in ages past
who heard on every side but hate and scorn,
yet truly served a mystic brotherhood.
I gaze on long-past medieval times.
This man, whose form has risen from your head,
is filled with inner pain each time he finds
himself exposed to man's ingratitude.
And yet he knows that there is meaning
in all that he experiences.
He looks toward this brotherhood of knights
and finds his destiny akin to theirs,
though they took persecution on themselves
intentionally, to plant a future seed.

(*Stratham, becoming Simon the Jew in Celia's vision, kneels down, his
arms open in prayer. Meaghan, becoming the deceased Supreme
Grand Master, stands above him.*)

I see him lifting up his thoughts in prayer
and in communion with the leader of the knights,
Most Eminent Grand Master of the Templars
who looks upon the Jew from spirit realms.

This Master knight, with many of his order,
had suffered gruesome death courageously,
wrongly accused of heresy, perversions...
of sodomy and sacrilegious acts.
As he burned slowly at the stake,
he bore his torment with composure.
I can behold how th' solitary Jew
can feel the presence of the martyred knight
and hears him speak from spirit realms,
though he had never met him on the earth.

MEAGHAN and CELIA (*speaking together*)
"You've found a refuge here within this castle.
Now soon with this whole brotherhood, you too
will fall a victim to those powers of darkness
that draw their strength from evil, yet through force
of opposition, always serve the good."

CELIA
He speaks about a radiant Spirit Being
descending from the kingdom of the sun
and, in a human form, appearing to the senses
in order to be understood by human hearts.
He speaks of Christ,   – – –
who links world goals with human destiny.
But all at once a violent rage flames up
within the seeker's solitary heart.
He thrusts away the hand so lovingly
held out to him. I recognize that hand:
it lives again within this woman who
appears before you here. For at that time,
as leader of the knights, she spoke to you:

MEAGHAN and CELIA
"Though you have found me here in spirit,
beyond the gates of death,
your destiny does not allow that we
can fully understand each other now.
And yet, through many hard and painful struggles,
our paths will come together in the end.

What has been planted in your soul
indeed may for the present die.
But you have breathed the spirit light
and you will come to earth again,
and then bestow upon the world
what we intended in our work."

(*Meaghan and Stratham now return to their own posture and places.
The lights change.*)

MEAGHAN
Though they're incomprehensible and strange,
these pictures sound familiar to my soul.
As soon as they arise, they fade away,
but leave a strong impression in their wake.

STRATHAM
How can I hold these pictures in my memory
when sense existence covers them again?
My Astrid, I have need of you
to bring me my own power of feeling
as radiant warmth within my earth existence.

CELIA
And now I see how you both met again
in your most recent former life on earth.
But only when your spirit had departed,
and this soul still remained behind on earth,
could you work with her from across the threshold.
For after you departed from the flesh,
the man she was, allowed you then to work through him
for the completion of a major work,
the building of a temple.
You've called her to you now in this dark realm
to help you solve the riddle of your life.

STRATHAM
Your words pierce through me to my inner depths.
Oh Celia, all the toil of my thinking
could never find the fountainhead of life

without the light of highest wisdom
revealed through you through many years and lifetimes.
I'll dare to hear what you've revealed here
and summon all my inner strength
to hold it in my consciousness on earth.
O, my dear Celia, what are you beholding now?
What further message do you bring?

CELIA
My dearest Simon, you can shine your light.
But darkness threatens to engulf your work.
I see a radiant being in these times.
The time is now. − − −
That Being walks the earth in spirit, shines
his light, and many people follow him.
But you stand at a distance and resist
his invitation reaching out to you.
Unless you find your way to him, your work,
meant for the healing of humanity,
will only serve their rapid downfall.
You've conquered for yourself,
the power to reach the light.
You soon shall find the source of the True Light.

AHRIMAN
The light of truth on earth is burning me.
I must work onward there, but not allow
those who enkindle spiritual knowledge
to bring my working in the world to light.
What these three souls have learned here in my realm
they must not bring to consciousness on earth.
For when their sight can think me as in truth
I am, within their thinking will arise
part of the power that slowly will destroy me.
But, −
the soul force who could cultivate that power
is chained in darkness here.

CELIA
However much you goad and pester Simon,
I'll always be beside him; since we've found
each other on the light-filled paths of spirit,
we are united, whether life must lead us
in spirit regions or the realm of earth.

This soul who now appears beside him here and
Stella Sophia, now in spirit realms
together with her teacher Benedictus
will work with us to bring about
what you oppose in human earthly life.

AHRIMAN
I only hope that they will slowly be forgotten,
as people always, in their darkened turmoil,
forget their past resolves and other lives.
For everything that comes into existence,
deserves to be destroyed in the end.

STRATHAM
And yet will come what has to come about.

(End of scene)
(End of Act II)

Act Three

8) Schism

(A cafe in a major city in the Midwest. Troy and Michael Capstone are sitting at a table, immersed in a private conversation. Later, Joanna.)

TROY
I'm honored that you ask me such a question.

CAPSTONE
I've never known a love like this before.
I feel an unfamiliar warmth rise up
into my heart. I never felt this for a woman.
What Meaghan and I share is something else.
The question here is, what the consequences
would be, were I to act upon these feelings.
What matters is not that the congregation
could possibly reject and turn against me
or that I have been broadcast to the world
to represent morality and family.
It's in the eyes of God and not of men
that I stand to be judged.
I know I am alone in this decision.
So why do I feel that this has meaning
not only for ourselves and for
our congregation here, but for humanity?
The Bible says that for a man to lie with
another man is an abomination.
It is unholy and impure. And yet
I know that, in the Acts of the Apostles,
when Peter said the beasts and birds
and crawling creatures were unholy and
unclean and he refused to kill and eat them,
a voice from heaven answered "Do not call
unholy what the Lord God has made pure."
How can I make a choice that's truly free?
As Christians, by the grace of Christ, we live
by lovingly perceiving for *ourselves*,

within our heart, what we must do.
And not by following the laws imposed
by an authority *outside* ourselves –
not even by the Bible's laws of Moses.
In Christ, Mosaic law is done away.
By grace we are not under its control.
But blindly following our senses' cravings
is also not true freedom. I know that,
even through instincts and desires, God
pours wisdom's light into Creation and
our human life. But when our sensuous urges
conceal themselves behind a mask of pious words,
they can corrupt the will and make thoughts lie.
The light of truth that radiates from heaven
can never penetrate a soul
that's shrouded in a fog of wishful notions.
My thinking is not sound if it is driven
by passionate emotions and desires
and twists the truth for personal reward.

TROY
I trust your angel; and that God will guide you
and you will find your way to know yourself
in peace and wholeness. But I'd like to hear:
What does the Bible actually say?

(*Joanna enters, unnoticed, and overhears the following. Capstone continues with emphasis.*)

CAPSTONE
In letters to the Romans, Paul described
the deeds of those who turn away from God.
He wrote that men among the Gentiles had
"abandoned natural relations with the women
and were enflamed with passion for each other;
for men committed shameless acts with men
receiving in themselves the penalty
due for their error." It is clear that God
forbid this for the ancient Hebrew people.
Such actions went against His will.

The Law of Moses is explicit.
It's in Leviticus,
"And if a man lies with another man,
as he would with a woman, they have both
committed an abomination:
they surely shall be put to death;
their blood shall be upon them."

(*Joanna clears her throat.*)

TROY (*sees Joanna*)
Joanna! I'm so glad that we could meet here.
We get to see each other after all.
Joanna Thomason, the famous author,
professor, government advisor and
my sister. This is Michael Capstone,
the churchman I was telling you about.
I wanted you to meet each other, and
I hope that we can build a bridge
to somehow span the chasm
that can so easily divide us.

CAPSTONE
I'm glad that you could meet us here. I know
you have a busy travel schedule, giving talks
and autographs. Congratulations on
your book's success. It truly is a wonder
how you have brought your spiritual views
of God's creation and His heavens into
connection with the current world affairs,
and Man and nature, in a way that has
captured the popular imagination and
received widespread attention and acclaim.

JOANNA
That's very kind of you. I know that you
have other views than those upheld by
the Cultural Authority, which I
advise. I'm sure there's much
you disagree with in my book.

CAPSTONE
I find your thoughts intriguing. But if they
indeed prove true and valuable, they only can
rightly unfold themselves if they're
allowed to do so in full freedom, in
a world where they are not imposed.
For otherwise they will work evil,
no matter how much good they may intend. But
I know you do not share my opposition to
the power and authority of the United Union.

JOANNA
Not only do I not share your opposition,
but I would also like to show my brother
the futility of his joining you in your
resistance and to help him see the good that
world government can bring to everyone.

CAPSTONE
It's not that government is bad –
within its proper bounds.
It should protect the rights that God has given us.
But when it starts controlling
all aspects of our lives, it is a threat.
That's why there should be limits to it.
I think we need less government, not more.

JOANNA
Without a social structure, we'd have chaos.
The government is there to help us
improve the world for everyone.
The Cultural Authority already
is implementing policies that foster and
support good education and good health,
and good nutrition for everyone
and cultural life that honors and
respects all people. That is just
not something every family can provide

without assistance. There are many
who don't know how their children should
be educated. In a post-industrial
and complex world, no individual
does anything alone.
The people have to work together.
How else but through a government?

CAPSTONE
Through our own free initiative.

JOANNA
The government is our initiative.
We *are* the government. It *is* society.
We only need to share the right ideals.
The world is now united and we have
collective power to enact our goals.
Through this, ideas and spiritual insights
which you have rightly noticed in my book,
can also find their place.

CAPSTONE
I well can understand your good intentions
for implementing and enforcing social forms.
But who decides what's right and good?
Do you believe that people working for
the Cultural Authority have the
capacity and insight to discern
how every child should be educated?
A free relationship, between
a teacher and a student or
a parent and a child, honors the
unique, God-given talents each one has.
Each individual's a child of God.
At every step, the present government
hinders the individual in the
unfolding of his or her abilities.

Because it must treat everyone as equal,
it hates the individual. It says:
"Since we can only use a person who
behaves just thus and so, if someone's different,
we'll *force* him to *become* the way we want."
It seems United Union leaders think
that people can only get along
if they are told: "You must be just like this.
And if you're not like that, well then you will
just have to – be like that anyway."

JOANNA
I find some guidelines good and necessary.
The government's not perfect: it can make
mistakes. Policies develop over time.
If they are faulty, they can be improved.
The law's alive and it is always changing.
We can improve the regulations and
pass better laws. I am now able to
participate in this and help the process.
And I intend to serve as best I can.

CAPSTONE
The best of situations would result if
people were given a free rein and trusted
to find their own direction for themselves.
Now, naturally I don't believe, if we would
abolish all government tomorrow,
that the day after tomorrow there would
be no more criminals. But I know
one cannot by authority and force
educate people to be truly free.
It seems to me the way is cleared
for the most independent people when
force and authority do not get in their way.

JOANNA
But that would lead to anarchy and chaos.

CAPSTONE
What we have now is tyranny!
Our rights are being taken from us.
We're being told what we're allowed to do,
what we're allowed to think and how to speak and write,
which words we are allowed to use,
what we can eat or drink and how to educate our children.
And now our church is under threat
of being banned.
Our incense, candles, incandescent light bulbs
have already been prohibited.
Our Sunday school curriculum
is so prescribed now by the law, that
if we complied there would be no time left
for our own content – not to mention
the fact that some of what's prescribed
we find misleading and repugnant –
and there are serious penalties for not complying.
Merely the fact that we are Christians seems
to turn the law against us.
I've been interrogated twice now
about our beliefs
and about language in our ritual.
We have been told we have to change our liturgy
because it contains religious language
that some might find offensive.
And we've been ordered to perform our sacraments
in contexts where they don't belong.
We have already paid excessive fines,
and face the prospect of eviction.

JOANNA
I understand that this is very frustrating
for you. And I am sorry. But the laws
and regulations you have mentioned must
have some intended basis in
legitimate concern for social health,
for safety, cult'ral tol'rance and well-being. But
I *will* look into this and see what I can do.

CAPSTONE
Perhaps it is the sin of pride that makes
you think you know what's right for everyone
and that the policies you think are good
should be enforced for all. In any case,
it is an error in your faith, a lack
of understanding, knowledge or belief
about the truth and truest freedom, which are
revealed and manifest in Jesus Christ.
This is what makes you hostile to the views
that I've expressed. And so our difficulties
will grow and increase more and more. We both
claim a relationship to spiritual truth,
and yet come into conflict when we
attempt to meet about the outer
conditions of our life. So there
is not much hope for harmony between us.
And yet I trust the wisdom of God's plan.
Careful reflection on all that we have said
perhaps may let you change
the opinions you had previously formed.

(End of scene.)

9) Ora et Labora

(The office of The Bridge of Christ. Meaghan and Stratham are sitting together in mid-conversation.)

STRATHAM
I'd thought your church would utterly reject him.

MEAGHAN
And where would we prefer that he would go?
Our church is called the Bridge of Christ.
It is a path for those who seek the truth.
We are all sinners in our wrestling souls.
We don't condemn your son for what he feels.
And only God can judge his earthly actions.
Everyone is welcome in our church
and to partake in our communion.
Your son as well.

STRATHAM
He doesn't know that I am here.
I rarely come to this part of the world.
But while I'm here in town, I had to come
to try to see what he is finding here.
A spirit longing guides my venturing
to solve a riddle that is haunting me,
and so I've come. Are you a pastor here?

MEAGHAN
I do sometimes conduct our services.
My husband also is a service holder here,
and he is usually our spokesman.
You may have heard of him. He's Michael Capstone.
He is away right now for a few days,
since I insisted that he take a break.
He'll be returning here on Thursday evening.
Perhaps you would prefer to speak with him.

STRATHAM
Perhaps one day I will.
For now it's you I came to see.
I sense that you could help me.

MEAGHAN
I'll do my best to try to understand.

STRATHAM
You may not know . . . My son's adopted.
His parents died soon after he was born.
We love him and we've raised him as our own.
My son and I are very close indeed.
He's always been a "keeper of the gate," a bridge.
And as a child he broke the mold and forged new paths.
We've tried to honor this, to value him for what he is.

His wanderings and healing impulses
have often been a catalyst for me
in my own destiny. It was because
of him my wife and I returned
to the community where I grew up,
so he could go to school there – with his sister.
And since he was a boy, we've been aware
he has a great capacity for love,
a warmth of soul that is unusual.
And when he grew to be a man,
he shared that love and warmth in many ways
that might seem strange or unexpected here.
And yet it seems that healing often comes
from what he does in life and in his work.
His words and deeds can truly ease the pain
in human souls.
But this religious streak . . .
I find it hard to understand.
It's always seemed to me religion lacks
what gives to human thought its firm support
and lends the sense of certainty to life.
And I was sure that churches would reject him.

MEAGHAN
Perhaps some would. Your son is welcome here.

STRATHAM
Do you have children?

MEAGHAN
No. We don't.

STRATHAM
I'm sorry.

MEAGHAN
It wasn't ever a priority.
And it's been possible for both of us to
devote ourselves more strongly to our work
and to pursue our independent lives,
supported by our deep and lasting friendship.
But what is it that you are seeking here?

STRATHAM
What you do here and what you represent
is something alien and inaccessible to me.
The worlds of spirit and the gods are real
to me, but churches and religious ritual
do not seem relevant to modern times.
That's why it's hard for me to understand
that he is so religiously inclined.

My wife would understand you well. She speaks
quite differently from me about the spirit,
and yet her work and mine shed light upon each other.
We have been blessed by many happy years
together in this life. – –
Her light shines gently onto every soul she meets.
And her work radiates with spirit light
far greater than my own. Perhaps you know of her
and her experiences of angels. Celia Gottlieb.

MEAGHAN
I've heard of her, but haven't read her book.

STRATHAM
Through her I've learned about Christ's cosmic realness.
But to experience him as if he were
a human being with us in life,
as Celia does − and Troy too in his own way −
is far from anything that I can grasp.

And now that Troy has found his way to you
and to your church, − − −
I'm at a loss for how to speak to him.
I hope that something good will come
of Troy's connection with your church.

MEAGHAN
It's what I pray for. −   −
Our ritual and the principles we practice
will surely strengthen his relationship to Christ,
to God, and also to his earthly father.

STRATHAM
I do appreciate your willingness to listen.

MEAGHAN
To listen is a part of what we practice:
Sit still, do nothing, wait for God to speak.
(*beat*)

STRATHAM
There's something else I'd like to share with you.
I have developed a technique
that people anywhere can use to heal
all kinds of maladies and problems in their lives.
Its popularity and widespread use
are growing rapidly. But suddenly
I'm plagued by doubt −
that these techniques could also be misused.

MEAGHAN
What do you mean?

STRATHAM
I wonder whether people will use the
techniques I offer to serve the good.

MEAGHAN
I've read your book. – – –
Your thinking seems like solid ground to stand on,
as long as you speak as a physicist
about the healing powers of mind and body.
And yet, when you are speaking of the soul,
I also wonder whom your work will serve.

STRATHAM
I hope it serves the human being – and our becoming.

MEAGHAN
Becoming what?

STRATHAM
                    Well, human.

MEAGHAN
                    And indeed,
our true humanity can be found only
in our Lord Jesus Christ, the Son of God.

STRATHAM
I wish I understood just what that means.
I simply don't experience Him as you do.
I cannot give my heart to Him unless
I feel a need for Him in my true being
and know within my soul his way of working.
For many years I've sought for Him,
but something always holds me back, defiantly
when I would turn to Him in faith.

The riddle that torments and frightens me
concerns my whole life's destiny:
All faith is drowned in doubt.

MEAGHAN
Have you applied your own techniques
to guide you in this quest?

STRATHAM (*deep breath*)
Even though I have this great resistance,
I deeply and completely trust
in the divine providence of
the world and my own human destiny.

MEAGHAN
And does your human destiny serve only
yourself, or do you choose to serve
a higher power, God or Jesus Christ?
We're living in the time of Second Coming, and
the Prince of Darkness, Antichrist, will soon set foot
upon the earth to make his final stand.
Could we pray? May I pray for you?

STRATHAM
Well. Of course.

MEAGHAN
Heavenly Father, thank you for your leading
Troy's father here to visit our church.
I ask that you be with him and protect
and guide his work – that it may serve you
to bring souls closer to you and your son,
Lord Jesus Christ. In his name we pray. Amen.

STRATHAM
I do appreciate that. Thank you.
My daughter, Joanna would be appalled.
That may be why Troy came here actually, in part.

(*They both smile*)

MEAGHAN
Much now depends on how we human beings
can find the way to meet each other's souls,
for we can often truly seem to be
like separate worlds apart, each one alone;
but if the gulf between us can be bridged,
great good may be created for the world.

STRATHAM
So you, an active leader in this church,
which is so different from our spirit path,
you would allow my stepson to become
a bridge from our community to yours?
In truth, it would be strange to join
your Bible-based religion with our spirit science.

MEAGHAN
To welcome your son Troy into our church
may be a mere beginning of God's plan
for what could weave between our world and yours.
And meeting you, I hope to learn much more
about your work and your community.
By valuing what each one's work can offer
unto humanity, we can collaborate,
and yet retain our own distinct uniqueness.

STRATHAM
There's something so familiar about you. (*beat*)

MEAGHAN
I'm sure that we have never met before,
although I've heard about your work and read
your book and therefore feel I know you well.

STRATHAM
It seems to me I saw you in a dream,
in some bleak place of haunting clarity.

MEAGHAN
The ways God guides his children can be strange.
If only we could know and understand.
But many wondrous things within God's world
are well beyond the grasp of human thought.

STRATHAM
And yet I have to tell you that I know
that you and I have met before on earth
in other lifetimes. I remember now:
I was in meditation in the spirit
and found myself within the dismal place
that has become familiar to my soul.
It is the realm the Lord of Darkness rules.
From there I have been able to extract
cold facts that then I use to serve my work.
Among the wandering unconscious souls
in this dark realm, *you* then appeared to me,
though I had never met you in this life.
And you were fully conscious and alert.
It seems that you had found me there because
we'd met each other on the earth before.
Two lifetimes passed before my spirit vision,
in which great deeds of world significance
were formed and wove between your soul and mine.
And I could see that we have worked together
when only one of us was living in the sense world.

MEAGHAN
(*stunned*)
Oh, my little soul,
what power divine is stirring in you now?
I've always thought that the idea
of many incarnations on the earth
was pagan heresy and truly nonsense.
But now, my soul is shaken by your words.

(*Meaghan and Stratham sink into concentrated thought. Luna and the Other Philia appear.*)

LUNA
Your truest self you find in Him
who guides the destiny of all
by softly calling from the future.
The force of His own being
He would lay down in your soul's soil,
to root your being in becoming,
that from the heights of spirit you unfold
the one you truly are.
Be bold enough to be yourself,
that you may offer up that self
as vessel for the Cosmic Self.

THE OTHER PHILIA
In weaving of your own soul life
within the deepest feeling,
so quietly in intimated whispers,
and in the brightest spark of light
in darkest chasms of your soul; when hope
arises at your moments of despair:
He's there, the I within your I, in you,
much closer to you than you are yourself.

MEAGHAN
I feel the presence of the Being of Love,
The Christ who one day will make all things whole.

STRATHAM
The forces of my soul reveal to me
what I am lacking. – – –
I cannot find my way into their words.

(*The soul forces disappear.*)

MEAGHAN
Surely my husband's guidance could assist you.
I now suspect that Michael's happiness
is intertwined, not only with this church's destiny,
but also with your own.
What we enact in our communion service

is of significance not only for ourselves.
In future times in many languages
our sacred ritual of offering
shall be enacted for the world's becoming.
This has been Michael's foremost goal in life.
His strength seems nearly lamed by opposition
that we now face from government officials
and from the ever-changing rules and codes.
But when your son came and befriended him,
he was rejuvenated, a new man,
and full of joy and happiness. It seems
that he has value to his life again.

But how much longer will our church exist?
The Christian world is being torn apart.
Our rituals may soon become forbidden.
I see no other possible solution
than if a bridge of trust could now arise
between our church and your whole sphere of life.

STRATHAM
Though I can see how you and I have been
connected in the past, a dark abyss
now opens up between us here.
Although I'm nurtured by the love and faith
that Celia experiences
through visions of the angels and the Christ,
I cannot find that faith within myself.
I've gained ability to shine my light
in spirit realms. And I can penetrate,
with my own power of thinking,
into the hidden frozen realms
of darkness where deep mysteries –
in the cold clarity of thought –
can often be revealed to me.
And yet I cannot find my way
to meet within myself that Being of Love.

MEAGHAN
Thoughts claiming to be drawn
from heav'nly wellsprings –
and yet resisting unity with others
flowing from the self-same origin –
can only seldom hope for harmony.
And yet it may indeed be possible
for those devoted to the will of God
to work in partnership if they can learn
from Holy Spirit what existence means.

———

You are much closer to Lord Jesus Christ
than you yourself are yet aware.
Your spirit soon will find
what ardently your soul is longing for.

(*End of scene*)

10) Sacred Burning

(*Troy's temporary apartment in the Midwest. Stella Sophia's ashes are in an urn on the mantle. Michael Capstone and Troy.*)

CAPSTONE
What is that sitting on the mantle? Or
(*slowly realizing*) should I be asking "who"?

TROY
                    – Stella
Sophia founded our community
back east. I brought her ashes with me.
I thought that she would want them buried here,
planted as something for the future. Now
I think they should be buried with the past.
Ashes are what is left behind, from burning. –
You were talking in your sleep last night.

CAPSTONE
Was I?

TROY
          Well, yelling actually.
It sounded like "Uhh, burning! Burning!"

CAPSTONE
It happens nearly every night now.

TROY
                    What?

CAPSTONE
That I have this recurring dream:
a temple burning; domes engulfed in flame.
I'm trapped inside, trying to hold it up and save it,
reaching through smoke at colored windows,
grasping collapsing columns carved in wood
or flowing shapes and swirling molded forms.
Or I am standing in a crowd,

helplessly watching from outside.
But always and more and more
I feel that I'm responsible –
that I created or constructed it –
its shapes and forms – and that
somehow it's my fault that it's burning.
The pain of that is terrible to bear.
It is as if I'm burning up with it.
Within it. – – –
It's obviously a picture of our church,
the current situation and my sense
of a responsibility and guilt.

TROY
Shall I tell you what it is?

CAPSTONE
What do you mean?

TROY
The temple. Shall I tell you what it is?

CAPSTONE
Please. Do you have anoth'r interpretation?

TROY
It's from your former life. It actually happened.

CAPSTONE
(*Pause. He takes this in.*)
Do you believe in, in reincarnation?

TROY
I can see people's past lives.

CAPSTONE
I don't know why, but
I find that really frightening.
You're telling me that it is true,

That I have been responsible
for the destruction of a temple
that I had helped somehow to build?
Lord God, give me the clarity
to see the truth and strength to bear it.
So you believe in Jesus Christ?
And also in reincarnation?
That He died for our sins,
but that we live again on earth
and face the consequences of those sins?
How can these concepts work together?

TROY
I don't know.
I don't see any contradiction.
And I don't try to understand.
My sister would have some
elaborate explanation,
but I love Jesus Christ. I really do.
I love the story and I know it's true.
I love the way he talks to people,
to each one individually, uniquely;
his words and deeds, especially his healings,
and how he gives himself in sacrifice,
the way he chooses to go through with it.
I don't know how to put it into words, but
he's very real to me. He's there. Always . .
more real to me than you are, or this room.

CAPSTONE
You have such freedom in your soul.

TROY
I do?

CAPSTONE
You've brought such joy and life into my being,
and opened up my depths of soul.
I think I've never *met* someone like you.

TROY
God knows I've never met someone like *you*.
(*beat*)

CAPSTONE
So, what else do you see?

TROY
What do you mean?

CAPSTONE
You said you see some people's former lives.
I am afraid to ask what else you see.

TROY
Well, usually I see a kind of picture
of someone standing just behind a person,
and then another image behind that,
and then another, and another –
way back to the beginning.

CAPSTONE
        The beginning?

TROY
                M-hm.

CAPSTONE
You see past lives clear back to the beginning . . .
of time?

TROY
        Yes.

CAPSTONE
                When God *first* made human beings?

TROY
I guess so. Yes.
It's more like countenances of each life –
not whole scenarios. But this is different:
somehow I know your dream is true.
And yet, if I look now – I can
see visages of many lives behind you.

CAPSTONE
Oh, my soul. (*pauses, closes his eyes for a moment, takes a deep breath*) Hm. Tell me. (*breath*) What do you see?

TROY
A history professor back in Europe;
A medieval Knight
who has abandoned wife and children;
A woman in a convent, writing plays and legends;
A Druid-Christian priest;
A teacher of philosophy in classic Greece;
A royal hierophant in ancient Egypt;
A sensuous, chaotic youthful hero,
bestowing wine and revels
in prehistoric times;
And in Atlantis,
a radiant being in
the temple of the sun.

CAPSTONE
(*looks at him*)
                    If God himself
were to descend on me in wrath right now,
within a wildly raging storm,
his fearful power could not frighten me
with more appalling terror
than what you have just said to me.
And yet I know you speak the truth.

(*End of scene*)
(*End of Act III*)

Act Four
11) In Christo Morimur

(*A meeting room at the office of The Bridge of Christ. The Board of Directors is meeting: Michael Capstone and Meaghan Gerald presiding; Blythe Truegood, Thea Twist, George Battle and Raymond Gumption. Silence. Peaceful, somber atmosphere. Later, Joanna and the spirit of Benedictus. Then Lucifer and Ahriman. Lastly, Luna and the Other Philia.*)

RAYMOND
From what you say, I think we have to face
the grim reality that stands before us:
there is a possibility we'll have
to discontinue our religious work.

CAPSTONE
(*nods reluctantly. Almost inaudibly*) Yes.

BLYTHE
And what about the businesses our members
have established to yield the church support
and spread the Word? Will they be under threat
from the authorities as well?

MEAGHAN
Quite probably. Unless they serve
their customers in secret, or these forces
that wield control are somehow overcome.

RAYMOND
Although they draw their strength from evil,
these forces, by creating a resistance,
will, in the end, promote the good.

BLYTHE
There seems to be no possibility of
somehow appeasing the authorities.

THEA
We must endure what heaven has in store,
however dark. And yet it seems unjust.
Is it no longer possible to have
a free society on earth?
Is that old document now meaningless,
that made it possible to some degree
for centuries upon this continent
to limit governmental power?
I won't complain about what God has giv'n us,
but I would like to understand His plan.
For how can people find our Lord and Christ
in such a world where freedom is constrained?

MEAGHAN
The strange vicissitudes of world destiny
are linked most wisely with God's plan,
as are the seeming contradictions of the
circuitous paths of individuals.
A good man in his hindered striving
is well aware of the right path.
For human beings still can make mistakes
whenever they are living on the earth,
but in God's time, they'll find their way to Christ.

CAPSTONE
Within our congregation, one can serve
the whole community with mind and heart,
although one's life is not unblemished.
We are all sinners in our struggling souls.

RAYMOND
The erring course of heart and mind − and body −
can make amends through service to the whole.

MEAGHAN
Our church has always welcomed those
who lack full purity of soul,

to take part in our consecrating service.
And if we cannot hold our rituals,
then God will find another way.

RAYMOND
Whoever serves the Lord and His true church,
weighs good alone in human souls
and so allows their sins to find atonement
within the course of heav'nly justice. But
we must not redefine our sacraments
and change our holy liturgy to fit
the moral edicts of the world leaders.

BLYTHE
I understand.
Our rituals cannot be changed since they
were given by the holy spirit through
the mouths and pens of our founders.
(*to Meaghan and Capstone*) But can you tell us more
about our situation with the law?

MEAGHAN
We've been officially accused of speaking,
within our ritual, in words and phrases
that some may feel to be offensive speech.
And we've been ordered to make changes
in order to accommodate divergence,
and to conduct our rituals for anyone who asks.
Police are now enforcing regulations
for the equality of cultural life.

GEORGE
Have we been contacted by the police?

CAPSTONE
Police are acting in the name of safety.
They're cracking down on open flames and candles.
They are enforcing mandatory treatment
with medicines the government requires.

Authorities are claiming ownership
of property held by religious groups
that do not follow regulations. So,
it's possible that we could lose this building.

(*slight pause*)

MEAGHAN
We must accept with joy whatever comes ...
"Not our will, but the will of God be done."

(*Blythe, Thea and Raymond begin to go out, but pause a moment as
George speaks.*)

GEORGE
Those words resound in all our hearts.
But what about the hatred that is spread
by the Regime and by its ideology,
the prejudice against all that is Christian.
Whole generations now are raised
without one bit of knowledge of the Bible.
And what they learn of Christians in the school
curriculum turns them against us
and closes many hearts to th' Word of God.

MEAGHAN
What we have planted will bear fruit in future.
We need not think of our work's ending, but of
fulfillment of our goals in later times.

(*Blythe, Thea, George and Raymond exit. Meaghan and Michael Capstone remain.*)

CAPSTONE
You speak of future times and planting seeds.
So could it be our souls will live again
on earth as human beings in the future
and bear the fruits these seeds have planted now?

MEAGHAN
Michael, you know that I've opposed the thought
that souls return to live again on earth.
I know the Bible speaks of an eternal
salvation with our Lord in heaven
after we die, or of eternal shame
in outer darkness and the lake of fire.
But I've been thinking of some passages that
seem to refer to other earthly lives.
The Lord's disciples asked him if a man
had been born blind because of his own sins,
which would imply a former life on earth.
And John the Baptist told the Pharisees
that he was not Elijah, but I wonder:
why did they ask unless they meant that he
had lived on earth before? And Jesus said,
"Elijah has already come," – that he'd returned.
I've prayed and prayed about it and
the answer I hear speaking in my heart
is that there is no conflict in these thoughts:
of Christ as Lord and many lives on earth.

CAPSTONE
I can't explain the meaning of your words.
And yet they open up for me a wide
and gaping chasm, an abyss in which
a spell that frightened me remains unsolved.
I hardly know now who I am. –
And yet I trust the Lord will guide my way
to a clear comprehension of the truth.

(*They go out. Joanna enters and is met by George Battle.*)

GEORGE
Ms. Thomason. It is an honor to
have such a well-known author visit us.
But, I must say, I am surprised to see
you here. You have not spoken kindly of us
in media or to the authorities.

JOANNA
I hold all human beings to be my friends.
That is a guiding thought I try to live by.
Yet it may seem indeed unkind
and even hostile to you,
that I hold very different views from yours.
I'm here by obligation as a sister
and as a friend. I know my brother, Troy,
has found his way into your hearts and has
become quite active in your church. For his sake,
I've come to warn you that your church is under
close scrutiny by the Cultural Authority
and it could soon be closed. If you are found
to be in violation of the law,
your rituals and your activities
will be forbidden and shut down.
Now I must ask you to
release my brother from your influence.

GEORGE
I well can understand, our ways seem strange
to you. I cannot be a spokesman
for our entire congregation:
But the church is a place for sinners, and
your brother came to us of his free will.
He's surely finding strength within his soul
to live increasingly with Jesus Christ
who frees us from the weight of sin.

JOANNA
I'm well aware of your ideas of sin
and punishment in hell for those who don't
accept your stringent reading of the Bible.
If you insist on judging Troy – that is,
his way of life – and try to change him,
I might be forced to use my influence in
the government against this church.

GEORGE
Since we are not aware of anything
we've done that could legitimately
be called a crime, in fact we're certain
of our unalienable rights,
we'll calmly wait to see if you will feel
obliged to add injustice to your cause.

JOANNA
You must ascribe it to your stubborn will,
if I am now compelled to other means.

GEORGE
It is well known that we oppose the
government's efforts to control our lives,
depriving us of our religious freedom
and other numerous God-given rights.
(*Slight pause.*)

JOANNA
I've said what I came here to say.
Would it be possible for me
to speak with Mr. Capstone?

GEORGE
You'll have to wait a while.
But I will ask him to come here
and speak with you as soon as he is able. (*George exits.*)

JOANNA
Strange to be in this place. It's interesting
to get a glimpse into this church that is
indoctrinating Troy. What I heard
his pastor friend reciting to him shows
what a fanatical religious cult
this is. Just being here fills me with dread.
I feel the fierce dark adversary's power
working here. Ahriman! I know
you're trying to lay hold of me with fear.

But I defy you! Oh. What is happening?
The horror grows . . . (*The Spirit of Benedictus appears*)
Angels, stand by me now!

BENEDICTUS
Listen, Joanna!

JOANNA
Benedictus! You, here in this place?

BENEDICTUS
I've often come to you and have been near you
when you were meditating, working on your book,
and inner striving carried you to spirit worlds.
If you can summon up the courage now
to hear the truth, the web of darkness spun of lies,
which threatens you, can still be banished.
So hear with courage also in this hour
what you must bring to clear cognition,
if spirit light in place of darkness
should now hold sway within your soul.

JOANNA
Oh, Benedictus, when I've sought for guidance in
my work and on my path, I sometimes felt
your presence in the spirit. You, our teacher – who
so generously shared your guidance and your wisdom
with all your pupils while you lived on earth –
you spoke to me from higher realms,
enlightening my mind and strengthening my knowledge.
Now in this hour I will devoutly listen to the revelation
that flows from you into my soul.

BENEDICTUS
You condemn this church, seeing in it all that we oppose.
You find support for this in words I spoke myself
while I was still on earth.
But you do not imagine that these words
can only hold the living truth

so long as they are rightly acted on
by those who are successors in my work.
So let those thoughts that I once held on earth
rise up afresh and live within your soul
in harmony with needs of newer times,
and see this church that seeks to understand the Christ
as I would judge and look on it myself
if it had been my lot to dwell on earth
and work with you today. – –
You've not yet recognized that I myself,
from spirit realms, when I had left behind
the earthly form in which you know of me,
worked actively to help the founding of this church.
And even now I work with them in spirit.

These individuals who join
such a religious movement truly are
seeking within their heart to find the truth
and to devote themselves unto that God
who once became a man and conquered death.
Many of them are able to perceive
his presence in the sphere of life around the earth
and hear his voice, calling from the future. He
appears and gives much strength and council
to people who know nothing of our views
and our demanding path. – –
Do not begrudge that they hold fast
to ancient written words or ways of worship
and do not know our spirit science.
We all contribute to the same good.
Only by peaceful union of the aims
sought by our movement and by theirs
can good be made to blossom on this earth.

JOANNA
How can I act on this advice? It differs
astoundingly from all that I have held,
up to this moment, to be right and good.

BENEDICTUS
I can direct you to the rightful path
if you will let the words I spoke on earth
take hold of you within your inmost soul.
And if you then will search for those words' power
within these worlds where you can see me now,
the rightful path will be revealed to you.
A further counsel I must also bring,
about the World Authority and your life work.
You have been . . .
(*He seems to fade away as Lucifer appears.*)

JOANNA
Your final words I could not comprehend.
They are obscured to me, for other beings
are drawing near, – – –
weaving a veil that hides from me your message!
Why do they come and stand beside you now?

LUCIFER
I bring you reassurance and protection.
Your path of spirit knowledge
and your inner work
have rightly guided you in this.

JOANNA
I recognize that it is Lucifer
who now appears to me within this place.
He often seeks to lead the soul astray.
And yet, through powers of grace, redeeming rays
of light shine lovingly within my soul.
I will admire, but not succumb to him.

LUCIFER
The error of this church's fellowship
is dangerous, because it speaks the truth,
and yet expresses it in such a way
that makes the truth more deadly than a lie.
A man who openly avowed he lied
would have to be a fool if he believed

that human beings would follow where he led.
Of course the Bible speaks of age-old truths,
revealed in the course of time.
But those who hold dogmatic'ly
to revelations of the past,
are not the ones to lead into the future.
These people claim that they are Christi-ans,
but they know nothing of the Cosmic Christ.
They merely follow sentimentally
their own group soul,
mistaking it to be the Son of Man.
And thus they lead themselves astray,
believing only *they* can see the truth.
My brother Ahriman, however, then
takes all their worship gladly for himself.
The human heart can best be led astray
when th' name of Christ is giv'n to Antichrist.

JOANNA
Oh, – he speaks with utter clarity
what I have often thought and said myself.
If Lucifer can praise what I believe,
then must I prove it to myself
that I've been wrong?
How shall I find the paths that lead to good,
if they are praised by Lucifer?
How can I unravel his argument
and see that Benedictus speaks the truth,
or whether I have understood him rightly?
The paths of soul must lead into confusion
when we desire to follow stubbornly
the concepts held to serve our own desire.
Has my own self conceit
misled me to oppose this church?
I must arouse within myself
the patience to await, completely tranquil,
what Benedictus' wisdom can reveal
to guide me still to understand the meaning
of his words, so dark to me.

(*Ahriman now appears as Benedictus, and Joanna fails to make the distinction.*)

Oh, Benedictus. You return.
I have dispelled the power of Lucifer.
What further message do you bring?

AHRIMAN
This further message comes from higher realms.
I'll lead you on your path if you will just
hold fast the words that I once spoke on earth.
Take hold of them within you: don't let go.
And with the power of these words of mine,
kill the thoughts that seek to lead astray.
Stand firmly on the earth;
I will reveal the rightful path to you.
You seek to work with the Authorities
to unify humanity. And rightly so.
Through world government,
our teaching can be spread throughout the earth.
And with the firm support of the authorities,
all culture will be rightly guided
through centralized communication from one place.
So conflict and confusion will be crushed.

JOANNA
Yes. I will continue to work closely with the government,
which seeks to bring diverse humanity
into a unity, to treat all people equally.
And I will also seek to find within myself
the way to work in friendship with this church.

LUCIFER
This church's so-called morality
is mere hypocrisy.
They say that they accept your brother as he is
and yet condemn as sinful what he does
in privacy with love for their own leader.

They seek division,
but the world leaders seek to unify.
True tolerance does not lie in judging
other human beings.
But in treating all men equally
and by enforcing rules protecting their equality
and safety for the good of all.

AHRIMAN (*now appearing again as himself*)
It cannot be an easy thing for you
to accept what Benedictus says about
this church. –
But what he says about world unity,
you know to be the truth.
Listen to him about th' Authorities,
but not to what he says about the church.
Reflect – he dwells now in the spirit world.
What works toward law and duty there, sheds light
for present situations only when
it is in line with current earthly circumstances.
He sees the future goals of all humanity.
But if at present you would act aright,
be guided also by what reason
and the senses teach.
Benedictus is a great initiate
whose thinking penetrates into all matters
of human earthly life.
Of course, it's true that human beings
should have a right to choose what they believe
and to speak freely.
But none the less it is not for the church,
or anyone, to speak in ways that are
offensive. You've discerned with clarity
how this church holds to the idea of sin,
which the whole world, in tolerance,
has now rejected as a silly concept
from the past.
You know that the authorities
seek to enforce equality for all,

and that this church opposes this.
Now that you know these things about this church,
how can you wish to live in peace with them?
For error is a barren soil
and good fruit does not ripen there.   *(Ahriman and Lucifer exit.)*

JOANNA
Here foll'wing Lucifer, now Ahriman appeared to me,
who also always seeks to lead astray.
How *can* I find the paths that lead to good
if powers of evil praise what I uphold?
It almost seems to me these powers of evil
are speaking truth and serving what is good.
And that this apparition of our spirit leader
was a deception and not Benedictus,
or that there is an error in his words.
Am I to hold to everything
that has been clear to me for years?
Or must it all come into question?
Was I misguided in my opposition
to this church, − −
but right to work with the authorities?
Or must I see the truth in the reverse.
Whichever way I turn leads to confusion.
− − I feel the earth dissolving
underneath my feet when I attempt
to see my way ahead on paths of thought.

LUNA
Though doubts are wrestling in your breast
and seek to give you over to dark depths,
your self will strongly battle its way through.
When powers of the heights have shaken you
and spirit forces shrouded you in dread,
you will sustain yourself.
Do not despair or feel that you are lost.
The strength in you still holds you firm,
so you can find your way
to clarity and truth.

OTHER PHILIA
As hopes that come to life in you,
you have preserved, within your present life,
the many fruits of your past life on earth.
Through heartfelt deeds and threads that karma spins
and through the power of love within your soul,
you will not lose yourself.
Within you, Love unfolds your being.
Oh feel this power of love in you
so that through it you will
behold yourself in truth.

(End of scene)

12) Empty Tomb

(The room or study of Marcus Lilly at the Temple Monument and
Archives in Europe. Marcus Lilly, the spirit of Stella Sophia.)

MARCUS
What Celia Gottlieb heard from Miss Sophia
at her memorial in America
still echoes in my soul. She seemed to speak
of wakening a Temple.
The Powers of destiny have laid on me
the task and the responsibility
for watching over and administ'ring
this temple monument and archives.
I have maintained and cultivated here
a knowledge of the work of Benedictus.
I have protected, from distortion and misuse,
his words and deeds. Defended accuracy
in quotes and in reports about his life.
I've given talks in many places in
the world, and I think that will still continue
even as the Authorities control
and limit travel to protect the earth.
And I have helped Joanna with her book,
which has received acclaim and opened up
an influential place where she can share
what spiritual science has to offer.
And yet
I know that Benedictus meant this place
to be a vibrant heart for spirit research,
a place where many people come and go
in active colleagueship and work.
Before his passing, Benedictus sought
to guide the intimately weaving threads
of destiny among his pupils, in
a mystery school within the temple here.
The temple was consumed by blazing fire.
His pupils fought and bickered, then dispersed.

(Ahriman appears in the background and slowly crosses the stage, unnoticed by Marcus.)

But then this monument was built.
And all my efforts to enliven it
have brought it only death.
Occasionally people come and go,
curious about what once was active here.
Stella Sophia used to come each year
and share her wisdom and experience.
And Troy unfurled his warmth and healing forces.
Now both are gone. This place is like a tomb.
The science of the spirit should
be bearing fruit for all humanity
in every walk of life and field of work.
Why can I not perceive within my heart
the way to lovingly enliven what
should flow out of this Temple to the world?
I gaze unsteadily at world confusion.

(Ahriman exits.)

I can't ascend to brighter heights of truth.
Why am I so bereft of spirit wisdom?
I only have the power to *comprehend*
the teachings about soul and spirit realms,
but not to see or enter them myself.
How can I understand this riddle of my soul?

(Stella Sophia appears)

STELLA SOPHIA
My dear Marcus.

MARCUS
Oh. Miss Sophia. You are here.
I can perceive you.

STELLA SOPHIA
Indeed. So strong for me your love is and
your sense perception's grasp of my true being,
my Self in spirit now you can perceive.

MARCUS
I recognize you on my soul's horizon.
In peaceful stillness I will listen,
patiently awaiting spirit certainty.

STELLA SOPHIA
Such spirit certainty you had
in your most recent former life.
For your own good and further growth,
these powers, by fate, were taken from you.

MARCUS
I've often had an inkling that a soul-
and spirit-strength had once been granted me.
And that I've lost a former power to see,
and to illuminate the realms of darkness,
to know the spirit world and to help others.
Do powers attained within one lifetime,
not carry over to the next?

STELLA SOPHIA
"Many a human being walks the earth
who would behold with bitter shame
how little in his present life there is
that corresponds to what he did before."

MARCUS
These words strike deep within my soul,
and echo as a haunting riddle,
resounding from my very self.
Will it be granted me to solve
this riddle and to serve?

STELLA SOPHIA
You'll find this riddle's burden if,
with inner strength, your own heart's power
of sacrifice you can arouse
to shine your light into a dark place where
your sister soul, whose destiny to yours
is closely linked, has need of you.

He strives to share the best part of his nature
with his new friend, to bring full light of wisdom
from the darkness of his feeling.

MARCUS
But Troy has left our scientific path
of spiritual development and joined
a Bible church, where his new friend's a leader.
He's found his way into the heart of one
who upholds what we strive to overcome.
What can I possibly do for him now?

STELLA SOPHIA
Into a dark realm, Troy
and his new friend soon will enter – where,
according to primordial laws,
only the human being, but not the gods,
can go. He needs your help,
and for this help I ask you now.
If strength within yourself you can call up,
you will be able to create the light
that's needed in that realm. Go there.
And find your sister soul and his new friend
to whom by karmic threads you're also bound.
Into their warmth of love, your light must shine.
You once received a power from realms of gods.
So offer to the gods what now you can
entice from demons in that darkened place.
Humanity receives the light of love
when it springs forth out of the realms of gods.
The secrets springing from a realm of darkness
can only be received by gods
when offered to them by humanity.

MARCUS
I will call up that strength within myself.
My thinking will now penetrate
deep hidden grounds of worlds
and with its radiant light, illumine them.

STELLA SOPHIA
Your light you now may shine in realms
access to which the gods cannot attain.

MARCUS
I will prepare my heart for sacrifice
so that my spirit may bring forth the light
to find the souls within that darkened place
and off'r its riddles to the waiting gods.

(End of scene)

13) Wrenched Away

*(The office of The Bridge of Christ, and the home of Michael Capstone
and Meaghan Gerald. During the scene, a monsoon-like downpour
and thunderstorm develop outside. Michael is sitting at his desk,
working or lost in thought. Meaghan is reading an official-looking
document. He does not see or hear her.)*

MEAGHAN
(Reading to herself or to the audience)
"Your church is now in violation of
the code for practices and propaganda.
In contradiction of subsections twenty
dash thirteen and eighteen dash twenty-two, which
define offensive speech, pursuant to
the Regulations of the Ministry
for Cultur'l Unity, Equality
and Fairness; in addition to
Safety Equality Directive Rules
and Regulations: lighting open flames,
Unsanitary practices:
drinking from a common cup,
offensive language, biases,
sev'ral discrim'natory practices,
exclusive rituals, as well as teachings
contrary to science and to common knowledge.
Public endangerment . . . Cease and desist . . . .
a violation of this order will result
in a police department action and eviction . . . "
So now it's clear: –
Continuing to celebrate our ritual openly
will put our congregation in grave danger.

(Deep breath. She looks at Capstone)

He's been so troubled lately.
For days he's been withdrawn and occupied.
I'll leave him to his quiet contemplation.

(She picks up Celia Gottlieb's book.)

I'll read a little here. This book may help
me find a way to face what threatens us.

CAPSTONE (*Alone*)
I feel an urging to escape
to a secluded life of prayer.
But when I take one step in that direction
in my thought, I see a specter of myself,
rising from the abyss and warning me:
"Truth does not resound within the soul
of one who only seeks a mood."
I see how easy it would be to fall
into despair. And oh, the pain:
confronting what my love for Troy may mean
and what it may inflict upon the church.
Now everything I am could just evaporate.
Uncertainty is everywhere –
whether our church will still be tolerated
or I be tolerated by the church.
Whether or when I will see Troy again.
I don't know how he got a permit
to drive a vehicle back east alone.
He said there's something there he has to do
and then he may go back to Europe.
But there is every reason to assume
that we will see each other sometime somewhere.
Since Troy told me that he saw
that I'd abandoned wife and children
in another lifetime, I have not forgotten it.
Whether it's true or not, it lives in me
as warning that our deeds have consequences.
And if it's true we live successive lives,
then we can learn from our mistakes,
make good the harm we've caused.
Lord God, the trials you put us through
are arduous and severe.
For I can see the lake of fire
in the outer darkness,
hear the wailing and the gnashing teeth.

Oh, is the love of Jesus Christ
still there for me? Will He show me the way?
Just yesterday, the sun was shining bright,
but now this downpour. I can hardly breath.

(*Light on Meaghan, alone, with Celia Gottlieb's book.*)

MEAGHAN
Were I to enter into spirit teachings
that go beyond our church's principles,
I'd need the guidance of someone who's won
my fullest confidence, because I've come
to understand her character completely.
This book by Celia Gottlieb moves me deeply.
Her words flame forth with gentle healing power
and enter actively into my soul.
I feel somehow I've known this power before.
Her vivid pictures and experiences
of Jesus Christ illuminate what many
who attend our church describe, though what
she says of angels and of other lives
I cannot grasp with my own understanding.
I asked Troy Fels, who is her son,
if he experiences some other life.
He told me he could see that I was once
a warrior monk and Christian martyr. –
I wonder how he knows or *could* know that.
Could it be true?   –   –
Again I'm stirred and shaken in my soul.

(*She crosses cautiously to Capstone. Pause. He notices her presence.*)

MEAGHAN
I have to tell you something you should know:
the final notice came from the Authorities.

CAPSTONE
I see. Well, we have been expecting this.
So now we know.

MEAGHAN
                 Yes, now we know –
Is that why you have been so sad and quiet?

CAPSTONE
Oh, Meaghan,   –   –   –
I think I have to share with you a sin,
a wrong that I have done.

MEAGHAN
                     What is it, Michael?
Surely whatever it may be,
we can bear it together, with God's help.
You shouldn't have to carry it alone.

CAPSTONE
The time I was away to take a break,
I spent those days and nights with Troy Fels.

(*slight pause as he tries to read her reaction*)

I've tried and tried denying and controlling this.
I know it is a sinful aberration.
But now I feel that I'm becoming whole
in ways that I have never felt before.
Sometimes we have to find our way through error.

MEAGHAN
Oh, Michael, I can see you clearly. (*She truly does.*)

CAPSTONE
Yes, Meaghan, you have often seen me clearly.
As mediator for the highest wisdom,
like a madonna, with your noble love,
you have enabled me to face myself
and parts of me I have ignored.
I know it's wrong. It is a sin and an
abomination in the eyes of God
and I'll receive within myself the penalty.

MEAGHAN (*now, not herself*)
So this is how we stand together. –
You married me in order to protect
yourself from such entanglements, but now
you use me to indulge your selfish cravings.
You married me, but now you rob me of
that marriage, tear me from my place in life.
Am I then nothing but a shield for your own pleasure?
A mediator for your vile so-called wisdom?
And not myself, a woman in my own true being?
No more will I endure this form of mine,
which is a mask and not the truth.

CAPSTONE
Oh, Meaghan, this is not like you.
It can't be you. Your eyes are dull.
Your body's movements are not yours.
Where have you gone?

MEAGHAN
You gave me certainty,
Yes, certainty, that now envelops me in doubt.
I curse your certainty,
and you I curse who made of me a tool
of those wild arts that have beguiled you
into depraved debauchery,
through which you seek to misguide men. –
Not for one moment have I ever doubted
your love and your devotion to our church.
Yet now one single instant has sufficed
to tear all faith in you out of my heart.
And I must recognize that the false god
you serve is but a hell-born demon.
I've been deceiving others in our church,
who've trusted you because you misled me!
I'll turn them all against you now;
we'll flee from you to where no deed of yours
can penetrate, and yet be near enough
so that our curses can still reach you!

You've robbed me of the fire of my blood
and given your false idol, your new friend,
what should be mine. The fire of this blood,
oh may it burn you! – – –
I thought that God led Troy into our lives
so you could guide his father. Now I know
that you and Tro-y were inflamed with lust
for one another. I believed your lying and deceit;
so you have made of me a fool.
We often worked together to defend
this church from enemies. So now let all
the power of those enemies destroy you
as you've destroyed me.
Let all that once was love for you and for
our church be changed into wild hatred's fire,
a fire that can consume you. Curse you! Cuh...

(She flails and collapses. He catches her.)

CAPSTONE
This is not Meaghan who is speaking here.
I do not see my partner, wife and colleague.
I see some hideous and dreadful demon.
Her Self is hov'ring somewhere else in spirit.
Oh, Meaghan, I've faced many trials. But now
you put me to the hardest test of all.

(He gently lays her on a couch and covers her with a warm blanket.)
Sleep peacefully, dear Meaghan.
I know that wasn't you who railed just now.
Your light-filled truest self soars forth
in blissful poise and bears this with composure,
while through your mortal semblance, left behind,
an evil spirit raged,
a vicious, jealous demon from the depths.
I cannot take these execrations,
spoken by your vacant shell,
as anything but Satan's craftiness. *(beat)*
For many years I've longed to understand
how knowledge of God's Kingdom can become
united with the body here on earth.

But this one instant has revealed to me:
the body is a temple for the spirit;
and when abandoned, it can be possessed
by darkest forces from the realms of Hell.

(*The lights change. The atmosphere becomes more inner, as Capstone goes into meditation.*)

A heavy fear is weighing down upon me.
An unfamiliar elemental power
now draws me into pictures like a dream.
I must make strong in me the power
to shed the light of spirit clarity
in realms of darkness and in unknown worlds.
With full-awakened thought, I pray,
God grant to me serenity
to strive for nothing –
and to wait in peaceful stillness,
accepting what may come –
and courage to confront myself. My soul
strengthens itself in spirit searching,
imbued with powers of thought.
An unsought mood awakens,
my inmost being filled with expectation.
I feel this solemn mood. – –
My senses silent, memory silent, too,
expecting only what awakes in spirit-
dreaming, within this solitude I will
await what gifts the Spirit may impart.
(*Lucifer suddenly appears behind him.*)

LUCIFER
You have indulged your urge for earthly pleasure
and stepped outside God's universal church.
You soon will read your book of life and know
the time has come that frees the single ego
from any group-bound spirit
and liberates your individual thought.
What if you *have* transgressed the church's path
and now could fall still deeper into sin?

You know the kind of spirit path that is
ordained for you is one of freedom.
True freedom is now possible for you,
but freedom to do good
means also freedom to do evil.
You've wrenched yourself away
from your religion's spiritual guidance
and fled into uncharted land, where you
have no one to rely on but yourself.

(End of scene)
(End of Act IV)
(End of Part One)

Part Two
Dispossessed

ACT V (Scenes 14 – 16)

14) Retrospective: The temple of a former Rosicrucian brotherhood

15) Retrospective: The home of Felix and Felicia Balde

16) The Realm of the Archangles in the Spiritual World

ACT VI

17) The Realm of the Green Demons

18) Church of The Bridge of Christ

19) Stratham's meditation room

20) The Monument and Archives

ACT VII

21) The Monument and Archives (continued)

22) Finns' home in the Sophia Community

23) The business offices of Gumption-Truegood

24) Government office

FINAL SCENE (Scene 25)

Spiritual Temple in the realm of life

Act Five

14) Temple Calling

*(The Temple of the Mystical Fellowship as it appears in Scene 10
of "The Guardian of the Threshold," Early Twentieth Century, circa
1914 or 1924. Benedictus stands in the East with Johannes Thomasius
– previous incarnation of Joanna Thomason; in the South, Capesius –
previous incarnation of Michael Capstone; in the West, the spirit of
the deceased Strader – previous incarnation of Stratham. Maria –
previous incarnation of Marcus Lilly; Felix Balde – previous
incarnation of Barbara Finn; Felicia Balde – previous incarnation of
Robert Finn; and the Nurse, the Other Maria, Maria Treufels –
previous incarnation of Troy Fels – stand in the center. The soul of the
deceased Theodora – previous incarnation of Celia – stands behind
Strader. Later, the Manager – previous incarnation of Meaghan
Gerald – enters and takes his place in the West, in front of the spirit of
the deceased Strader.)*

BENEDICTUS
The soul of Strader, sun-imbued, has, through
the strength'ning of his spirit powers, driven
the messenger of error into flight.
Though Strader now no longer works among us
within his body's sheath, as spirit-star
he'll shine upon the working of his friends
within this temple and in bringing spirit
revelation into earthly work.
You each according to your destiny
have met the solemn Guardian
who holds stern watch where two realms have their border.
And some of you have crossed His threshold.
The gateway to this hallowed shrine
is but a symbol of that threshold.
The brothers of this sanctuary have handed
over their offices and sacred symbols
to you, my closest pupils, who've attained
to spirit light outside this place's guidance.
The former holders of your offices

made manifest the power of spirit light
through ancient sacred customs. And you have,
in solemn reverence and devoted work,
honored these holy mystic rites. But you
have found your own way here through spirit worlds
and tests of soul in life. As you stand here,
you have brought something new into what's old,
which had so nobly ruled since earliest times.
Your benefactor, Hillary, lies ill,
who placed his fortune and his family business,
with all its resources, its reputation,
its properties and workshops, in your hands.
For many years he served here faithfully, as
Grand Master in this place, until his time
had run its course and a new age began.

JOHANNES
Our souls have joined together in this shrine
and sounded forth in rhythmic unison.
Our deed is now recorded in the Book
of World Destiny. What otherwise
would have remained as solitary being
awakens to true life, because our forces
willingly form a higher unity
here, in accord with measure and with number.
Each one of us makes fruitful for the others
the spirit light attained in our own souls.

BENEDICTUS
Maria and Johannes, you have now
progressed in seership to full-awakened spirit vision.
And you are moving boldly forward from
the life of mysticism to the world of sense.
The time has come when spirit light that rays
out from this sacred place is manifesting
in earthly work that's finding noble forms
as human spirits give to it their stamp.

JOHANNES
Our dear friend Strader's passing is a sign
through which the spirit's pointing out the way.
So we now welcome in our midst one who
had previously opposed our work but who
now proves our faithful brother in the spirit.
So let him enter now this sacred place
that he may join his work with ours.

(*Thomasius knocks three times, the Manager enters the temple;
Capesius leads him in so that he takes his place in the West.*)

Dear friend, within this place, which you have entered,
our modern scientific thinking
is compatible with sacred and primeval
knowledge. This consecrated place bestows
on you the blessing of the cross of roses.
The work you do, which serves our daily life,
shall here become a spirit offering
and so bear fruit for progress of the world.

BENEDICTUS
For many years it seemed quite clear to you
that spirit work within these sacred walls
must not be mingled with the practical
affairs of life, that industry and business
must stay aloof from spirit practices
and take their own course in the sphere of commerce.
But then your heart revealed quite other thoughts.
You have unlocked your soul in your own way
and come here to this temple now transformed.
Your management of factory offices
has made it possible to manufacture,
and to distribute, many useful products
that people find are truly beautiful.
The source of inspiration for these products
is cultivated by the spirit science
enlivened in our souls within this temple.
And so the friend of Hillary may serve
within this sacred place, for you have learned

to comprehend the spirit language that arose
in you when you first heard those occult words,
which can become a source of inner strength:

"And yet will come what has to come about."

For in a former life you nobly suffered
a gruesome death and conquered for yourself
your slumb'ring spirit sight. In *this* life you
had pressed yourself into a waking sleep.
But now you have awoken to the signs
by which the spirit gives direction.

MARIA
Through your participation here, our work
will link itself to pract'cal life within
the world of sense. Administration
will be imbued with esoteric substance.

CAPESIUS
For souls who seek for meaning, though they're fettered
by their material concerns of life,
you now are forging a new step upon
the path that leads one's own way to the light.

MANAGER
Following in Strader's place and with
the guidance of his radiant spirit light,
I stand now in the West where words I speak
wish to reflect our life in images.
Though thoughts arise quite unfamiliar to
this little soul of mine, with confidence
I dedicate my full capacities
and strength to carry out the temple's aims
through practical endeavor on the earth.

BENEDICTUS
You too, Thomasius, have gained new forces.
From realms of shadows you have freed
the youthful shade for whom, in time's deep womb,

Maria's soul kept faithfully the powers
you cultivate now lovingly for him.
As you begin to reunite yourself
with him and give him light, his breath can pour
illuminating strength into your aims.

JOHANNES
And I will not succumb to Lucifer's seductions,
for I have met that tempter face-to-face
and seen beyond his dazzling deceptions.
Though I may still admire him for his beauty
and I am grateful for his powers as
I work artistically, he will not work
as active force within my will.
Aware of the effect of temple words,
I stand here in the East where I endeavor,
according to the measure of my forces,
to render service to the spirit world
before this altar, symbol of the sun.

BENEDICTUS
Maria,
you have united your work with the temple.
The holy solemn vow that you have made
illumines here the path of earth salvation
and radiates its strength for mutual work.
Johannes is now free to stand
beside you as an independent soul.
And still your greatest trial is yet to come.
You know you are illumined by a god.
A higher being has descended to the earth
and taken up abode within your sheaths,
laying a seed-force in your being,
so spirit eyes could be evolved to waken in your soul.
That godly spirit guided you through many trials
and strengthened you in times of triumph too.
A great step forward in the world's becoming
is possible since this god has united
itself with you and with your deeds,

as mediator for new healing forces.
A time will come when this so lofty being
will leave you on your own, and you must find
the strength within yourself to see the way ahead.

MARIA
I will make strong in me
remembrance of the vow I made:
never to let myself be overcome
by th' bliss we feel when thoughts of ours grow ripe.
I have prepared my heart for sacrifice
so that my spirit only uses thinking
in order to bring forth the fruits of knowledge
as offering to the gods.

BENEDICTUS
                    Capesius,
the many-colored light now gives you strength
and fills you with its picture-bearing essence.
What now reveals itself to you in spirit,
is just as comprehensible to you
as what you grasp from your surroundings in
the sense world. So outer work will not
disturb your inner life. Your hopes
for earthly deeds may now be realized.

CAPESIUS
As is the way with sacred mystic work,
the one who stands here in the South
must humbly sacrifice unto the spirit,
here in this place where love should stream through wisdom –
as the sun's power streams warmly forth at noon –
upon what some call good and others evil.
Love treasures all and asks not whence it comes
but how to use what rises into life
from world depths, however it springs forth.

BENEDICTUS
And yet love often speaks with gentle words
and needs support in soul's foundations.

MARIA
We human beings, more than all other spirits,
are needful of that God who does not ask
for admiration but who radiates
His highest healing power only when
He Himself dwells within our inmost soul
and Who, in death, proclaims life lovingly.
When we can rightly understand ourselves,
we call out from our longing heart to Him:
The goal of Love for souls on earth, is this:
Not I, but Christ is living in my being.

BENEDICTUS
As long as your soul turns toward His Spirit
as you have vowed to do, – then Christ
will give this hallowed place of wisdom
His warming light, with spirit-love's true meaning.
This meaning weaves together many paths.
Mother Felicia and Father Felix
– Maria Treufels also, who
lovingly cared for Doctor Strader –
have reached the spirit light in other ways
and bring abundant riches with them here.

THE OTHER MARIA/NURSE
Love works its blessing only in the light
and so, in service of this temple,
I offer up my warmth of love
unto my higher sister's light
and lovingly repeat Capesius' words:
Love treasures all and asks not whence it comes
but how to use what rises into life
from world depths, however it springs forth.

FELICIA
Capesius often tells me of the true
Spirit sources of my fairy tales,
which have a motley independent life
as images that rise up of their own
accord within me. So I humbly do
my best to share my tales and puppets from
my inwardly illumined gift of soul,
though I can understand but little of
the ways taught here to reach the spirit's light.

FELIX
For many years, in my own mystic way
of life, I strove toward the spirit light
in solitary inner contemplation.
Although the words I hear within these walls
often resound from regions strange to me,
yet here my mystic path is opened up
to knowledge gained within the world of sense.

MANAGER
For me to step into this mystic temple,
I need the guidance of a man who's won
my fullest confidence, because I've come
to understand his character completely.
I've found that man in Strader. – –
I learned to comprehend the inner language
sounding from his soul.
When I first heard the words he spoke
as if they reached him from another world,
the spirit world laid hold on me. Those words
have never left my mind since Strader spoke them
so long ago to Hillary and myself.
And when he was transported into spirit regions
I realized I'd been touched by spirit sleep
that I had never noticed until then:
A glowing light illumined my whole being
and powers of vision wakened me.
From spirit regions, Strader spoke those words

again to me. Their power carried me
where I could clearly recognize him, not
his earthly being but the spirit in his soul,
who many hundred years ago in some
past life on earth could raise himself to most
unusual inner heights. And now, within
his occult words, my sense perception had
so firmly grasped the essence of his being
that I was certain, in the spirit realm as well,
that what I was beholding there was not
a phantom, – it was his own true being,
which I'd encountered here in daily life,
and which I now could meet in spirit.

"And yet will come what has to come about."

What is it that should come about? –
I'll join you in the quest to carry forth
the power of spirit into sense existence.
My destiny has shown me a stern face.
I see here in your circle and this temple
a knot my former thoughts could not unravel.
The power of fate that guides my thread of life
has given it a part within this knot.

(SOUL OF) STRADER
The soul that shines on you as spirit star
sends loving rays of light into your work,
endowing you with heartfelt power of thought,
revealing inner forces, so that you
are able to prepare yourselves
with greater strength for spirit deeds.

(SOUL OF) THEODORA
I was allowed to win this light for you
because you lovingly strove toward my light.
And when your time approached
to leave your body's sheath,
you gained the power to reach that light yourself.
Through you we can more strongly arm ourselves

to work as consciously productive
revealers of the spirit light.

STRADER
And living hope I'll flood into your souls
to build an earthly home for spirit deeds,
a place in which the light shall be enkindled
to radiate and warm the spirit worlds,
the light, which through our sense-activity
will seek anew a home in earthly life.

BENEDICTUS
A call sounds forth to you from spirit realms,
from which the soul of our friend Strader carries
into this karmic circle an intention.
The hidden myst'ries of this sacred place
have given way to *newer mysteries*.
The possibility is granted now to build
a Temple home for these new mysteries,
where earthly spirit work, encompassing
all fields of human life, will be endowed
under the symbol of the Rosy Cross.
I must myself be separated from this work
whose constitution must be grounded in itself.
I may be counted only as interpreter
of principles that flow from spirit worlds.
The sovereign independence of your striving
is absolute necessity in future.
My own well-being and development
depend on yours. − − −
The spirit powers who endow this work
ordain probations, trying souls who serve
and testing whether what has been endowed
can long endure, and whether freedom of
the spirit shall not perish from the earth.
In every age a temple of some kind
has manifested wisdom for its time.
And now those shrines will rise in a new form
in which the fullness of the human being,

together with realities of cosmic life,
shall be made visible, if you will choose
to dedicate your forces to this task.

JOHANNES
It's been my task till now to guide the workshops
built for us on Hillary's property
so that what is mechanically accomplished
is formed artistically to give nobility and beauty
to things of human daily use.
I will renew my dedication now
and happily devote myself to oversee
the work on the construction and design
of windows, forms and colored murals
for this new temple's walls.

CAPESIUS
The images of history and culture
that lived in me for years as mere illusion,
have given way to spirit certainty.
Now with Thomasius' artistic work
I can make manifest for all to see
direct perception of past times on earth,
made strong in me through pain of destiny.
Organic forms developing in time
will sculpt the columns, walls and cornices.
What lived as consciousness and cult'ral life
in ages past, and mankind's future aims —
speaking but softly from eternity —
will manifest in forms and images
within the newborn Temple of the Word.

THE OTHER MARIA/NURSE
I must admit I want to give
my faithful love and service to these plans —
that live so warmly in your thoughts —
for serpentine enclosing waves of wood
and arching, many-colored pictures, which
will work with healing love on human souls.

FELICIA
My fairy sprites and spirits now appear
well fashioned out of earth materials to
give joy and strength to children's fantasy
and also many happy hours to grown-ups.
With inner happiness, I see my fairy kings
and princesses, my air and fire sprites as well,
dance merrily on many hundred puppet stages and
in doll-games shaped with artistry.
Thomasius has beautifully crafted them
into mechanical, embodied dolls and puppets,
and they have found their way into the rooms
and nurseries of many, many children.
If now the fairy folk who show themselves
within my humble stories were to shine
in colored light of a new temple's windows,
these spritely spirit beings would not complain.

FELIX
That inner force that guides my steps, has led
me to this sacred place, which is related
to temples I have visited in spirit
as written words relate to sounds of speech.
If revelations of the spirit can
be visible in form and color
within an earthly Temple for our time,
then I will gladly be of service to it,
in whatsoever humble way I can.

MANAGER
Until this moment I've held back some news:
Regretfully, I must inform you that
some hours ago my friend and business colleague
Hillary Gottgetroy, crossed the gate of death.
   –   –   That we should build a temple,
a school and home for these new mysteries,
using the property and *re*sources
he left to us: This was his final will,
which filled his heart and mind at his life's end.

BENEDICTUS
Some people on the earth are called
by cosmic destiny
to sacred work for periods of time,
and destiny will give them other tasks
when, in this service, they exhaust their strength.

(End of scene.)

15) Powerless

*(The Balde's Cottage, some years later. Felicia, Capesius and Maria
Treufels, the Other Maria/Nurse. Later, the Manager, and the spirits
of Benedictus, Theodora and Strader.)*

THE OTHER MARIA/NURSE
I never really understood a word
that father Felix uttered. But by being
within his presence, I was always comforted.
And then your simple stories had a way
of making clear
whatever he was trying to express.

FELICIA
Although I know that he is with us now
and that his spirit lives for future deeds,
he is no longer here. – –

THE OTHER MARIA/NURSE
He lived a good long life and gave his wisdom
freely to all. He will be deeply missed.

FELICIA
He simply could not bear
to see our Temple burned
and then our fellowship dispersed.
He knew his force of life was running out.
He'd always had a sense for that in others,
and now he could perceive it in himself.

THE OTHER MARIA/NURSE
Without our teacher Benedictus here
to guide us, – we could not find our way.

CAPESIUS (*as in a trance*)
Benedictus now lives on in spirit realms.
He has been called to other deeds.
His mission here on earth

has had to end for now
because we failed him.

FELICIA
He sometimes talks like this,
though he is otherwise oblivious
to human beings or anything around him.

THE OTHER MARIA/NURSE
I well remember when he was like this
before, increasingly for ten long years.
But he recovered. And with strength
and presence he worked tirelessly,
envisioning the forms and images
the Temple building would embody.
And there he spoke with vivid eloquence
to throngs of listeners about our spirit science.
Oh, how I loved to listen to his words
and see his thoughts become artistically
embodied. Yes. He seemed indeed to have
extraordinary insight and new skills.

FELICIA
And now all that is far away.
He lives with his whole being
in other realms.

THE OTHER MARIA/NURSE
It grieves me greatly
to see him once again like this,
after so many productive years.
I grew quite close to him
as often we worked side by side.

FELICIA
I well remember that my Felix said,
when our Capesius was in this distant state before,
that his strange words and visions
could be relied on as the truth.

THE OTHER MARIA/NURSE
– – How strangely he now speaks
of our great teacher's death and of our failure.

FELICIA
It is almost unbearable to think
how Benedictus stood once on the earth,
among us in our work, his revelations
made visible within our Temple's forms
and colors. Now, all of it is gone.

(*Manager enters, noticeably disheveled.*)

Come in. You wish once more to see your friend.

MANAGER
Although it brings me deepest pain,
I cannot stay away. – –
Before he came to be like this again,
he often spoke to me about a growing
awareness of an ancient debt he owed
to Strader. And we vowed to find
each other once again on earth and work
to pay that debt together in the future.
But still, sometimes I feel somehow our work
could be revived yet in *this life*. But then
painful reality sinks in and I must see
what terrible mistakes I made:
I should have known that it would lead to ruin.
– – – Or was I right
to dedicate myself to spirit work
united with the practicality
of business?
I now no longer know.
My only solace is in drinking.
And that has now completely ruined me.

FELICIA
Come sit awhile with us.
Perhaps some peaceful guidance
will find its way to us.
The fairy sprites may whisper me
a tale that's seeking to be told.

CAPESIUS
Maria's spirit only loosely now
will dwell within the body's sheaths.
When Benedictus died, her spirit followed.
The godly being, who had shone
so brightly through her words, had to depart.
And when her own true being followed her
beloved teacher into spirit realms,
the Prince of Darkness then took hold
within her mortal body's vacant shell.

THE OTHER MARIA/NURSE
Oh dreadful. What a curse, if this is true.

FELICIA
I think that we can trust what he is saying.

THE OTHER MARIA/NURSE
How dreadful then. The Prince of Darkness
spoke through Maria's lips? – –
Then what she said and did was not her own.

CAPESIUS
Soon I will leave this earthly sheath.
Through many lives of chastity and abstinence,
I've been devoted to the spirit's work.
But one life filled with selfish craving
touched on unspeakable desires.
I could not bear to face that in *this life*.
But in my *next* life I must reconcile
with drives that I have long repressed, and cross
a threshold into realms of sensual urges.

The times are coming when humanity
will cross this threshold, consciously
or not, and regions that have been concealed
will be as present as the air we breathe,
revealed for all to see and struggle with
for better or for worse. – May gods
not turn away from us within this struggle.

(Benedictus now appears together with Theodora and Strader.)

Spirits are coming. They wish to speak to us.

BENEDICTUS
My work on earth has ended for the time.
I had to leave, to take up other tasks.
When I have built an altar in the spirit,
I will return; new myst'ries to unveil.
Till then the mysteries withdraw, in silence.

THEODORA
We will shed light,
in loving guidance,
on our friends –
and soon return
to help prepare the way.

STRADER
We'll find each other once again
beyond the seas –
and spirit work on earth
will come again.

CAPESIUS
And Felix and Felicia's son,
together with Maria's daughter,
begin already now to plant the seeds.
They've fled across the sea. – –
Through them the future work is now prepared.

MANAGER
How terrible to think that all we've done
has died. I cannot think
that it will come again –
another time, another land –
it is too much to hope.
Such dreadful words were spoken, such
horrible deeds destroyed all trust among
our brotherhood. Our fellowship has died.
Johannes Thomasius and Maria claimed
to be the true bearers of Benedictus' work.
But how could each of us be ostracized?
Beginning first with you, Maria Treufels,
who stood beside our teacher as he stepped
across death's threshold.

THE OTHER MARIA/NURSE
To understand Maria's cruel words
were not her own, may give me comfort. But,
I too said things I should have left unsaid.
But now the tragedy has passed;
it was of this life only.
We will unite again in future times.

MANAGER
The desperate pain is far too great.
I don't know how I can go on.
My drinking has to stop,
and yet I'm powerless
to take control of my own life.
I hear my friend here speaking strangely of
the spirit world. But all seems dark –
and only clanging noises sound to me.

FELICIA
What else is there for me to do but tell a story?
A picture has arisen in my soul,
which now would like to share itself with you.
And this perhaps can give some nourishment.

Once upon a time there lived a prince
who'd lost his crown, his scepter and his sword.
Through the enchanted gaze of a beautiful princess,
he had even lost his very self.
He wandered through the world aimlessly,
and ever and again he visited
the garden of the princess, whom he loved.
But he could never touch her or be near her,
for, though her gaze had robbed him of his spirit,
her touch could kill.
One day he stood again within her garden,
longing for her forbidden touch.
He could restrain himself no longer.
"If your touch kills, then let me die," he said,
and rushed to hold her tightly in his arms.
And when she reached to try to stop him,
she touched him that much sooner.
For a moment they embraced,
and then he fell upon the ground and lay
lifeless at her feet: The princess wept.
Try as they would, her friends could not console her:
The Prince was dead.
A green and magic snake encircled him;
a magic glowing lamp illumined him;
And then an agéd woman's basket grew and
carried him across a magic bridge.
When his beloved princess touched him once again,
the power of her spell reversed;
the Prince awoke.
A sword, a scepter and a crown were given him.
The Prince and Princess were united,
and a new day dawned.

MANAGER
Oh, little soul of mine. Out of the grief,
a brightly glowing light ignites in me.
I see my friends and even those who died
all standing round. And in the midst of all

of us that godly being speaks who once
as man has lived a life on earth –
the being of love, whom human beings most need.
He speaks to us. And I can hear his words:
"Fear not," he says. "For I am always there –
among you in your suffering.
If you will dare to love,
then comfort will arise
and all things will appear
as God intended them to be."
Oh now such peace as I have never known
fills all my being.

(End of scene.)

16) Healing Heaven

(The Realm of the Archangels in the Spiritual World. Benedictus, Michaél and the other Archangels. Later, Strader and the Manager, then Felix, Felicia, Theodora, Capesius, the other Maria/Nurse, Johannes and finally Maria.)

BENEDICTUS
Exalted Being of the Hierarchies –
who stand before the Christ as countenance –
Oh you, Archangel Michaél, who have
ascended to the realm of the Archai,
my life on earth has ended and my work
is incomplete; – – –
it has not borne the fruit that you had hoped for –
My friends, my pupils were not able to
take up the work. – They fell asleep.

MICHAÉL
(Speaks, though we cannot hear his sublime and earnest voice. Only an echo of music – perhaps cellos and horns.)

BENEDICTUS
No one, sir.
In the end I was alone.
I had to leave.

MICHAÉL
(Again, we cannot hear him speak.)

BENEDICTUS
Yes. I know.
Your brothers here have also turned away.
They have no faith in human beings.

(It gradually becomes apparent that six other archangels are standing in various places and postures behind Michaél, their backs turned to him and to us.)

I know they say that human beings have
rejected and abandoned them.
So I can understand that they
no longer seek to work with us.
I come here now in quite a different way
from how I often would approach you
while I was living on the earth.
When, on my pilgrimage of soul,
I had attained that stage that granted me the honor,
of serving with my counsel in your spirit spheres,
you came to me with other higher beings, who
wished t'unite themselves with human fate,
and who assigned to me the task to link
the deeds of heaven to human destiny.
I stand here now, speaking as one man alone,
one human being, reaching out –
to say to you that even if I stand alone –
there is at least one human being,
one humble heart
wishing to link the deeds of earth
unto the destiny of heaven; –
and looking to your realms –
perceiving you and offering
his conscious will to service of the good.
My destiny and my heart's power of sacrifice
have joined me with other earthly souls

(*Strader/Stratham and the Manager/Meaghan appear.*)

(*The other Archangels begin to turn.*)

who are still on the path.
And though they may at times have lost their way,
their deed still stands upon the earth.
The earthly temple burned,
that once made visible your realms and work.
And yet the deed that made it possible
can never be dissolved from world becoming.
My pupils stepped into the ancient sacred
mystery offices, took on the symbols
and the responsibilities. The ancient

mysteries are transformed and opened now
to modern human consciousness.
There is no going back.

(*One by one, Benedictus' other pupils appear: Felix, Felicia, Theodora,
Capesius, the other Maria/Nurse, Johannes and finally Maria.*)

Give us your blessing.
A human gesture humbly reaches out to you.

(*The angels gesture toward Benedictus blessing him and then his pupils,
then toward the audience, blessing us. The lights shift. Benedictus is
alone.*)

My mission on the earth has ended, for this time.
Yet still I have much work to do in other realms.
In spirit work there is no failure,
only diversion and delay.
The mysteries remain veiled.
They will remain still veiled until
an altar rises up in spirit worlds
that has been built in realms of sense,
a sacred place for human souls.
When such an altar can be consecrated
in fullest consciousness,
then can my work continue on the earth
and only then the mysteries will be
revealed for all of humankind.

(*End of scene*)
(*End of Act V*)

Act Six

17) Green Demons

(A great gateway to the realm of the Green Demons. Lucifer and Capstone. Later, Troy, Marcus, Robert and Barbara, the Other Philia, then Meaghan. Dark, shadowy realm, the walls or boundaries are alive and moving, undulating. The whole atmosphere has a green glow and smells of sulfur. Curved and rounded shapes in the landscape seem to rise and fall, surge and swell. *Gradually it becomes clear that these are beings or creatures.)*

(Lucifer appears with Capstone, outside the gateway.)

LUCIFER
Relying on yourself, you have compelled me
to bear you here on freedom's spirit wings
to stand before this odorous murky gate
that guards a world of gaping primal darkness
far from the realms of gods, where demons call
forth urges that create and can destroy.
You once united with the spirit worlds,
but now you would set foot into the darkness.
Your new-found friend has also willed his way here;
he seeks to solve the riddles of this place,
the mysteries of the flesh and surging blood,
with knowledge that he thinks has power to shape
itself to deeds on earth. He too has read
his book of life, and yours as well
and knows your actions in all former lives.
Thus shines a light through him that he believes
will now enliven conscious guiding forces
that can enhance clear-minded thoughtfulness
in gloomy chasms where no light has shined,
where motives rooted in blind instincts live.
But whether this or that succeeds
depends upon maturity of will.
His will is ripe and, like a fruit,
will soon be plucked. – – –

But you are not so easily confused
for you now see the errors of your life.
And your own light will guide your further steps
within the cosmic will, where I'm at work
as it streams mightily through human souls.
I make you truly human only when
you leave the darkness, and your inmost self
becomes illumined by the cosmic light.

CAPSTONE
I know you well. I'm grateful that you let
me feel my true humanity when I
can stand as Self within God's universe.
But, I will benefit from all your power
to elevate my soul to spirit heights,
only so long as grace of God upholds me.
And though I often can admire your beauty,
I will not let you live within my will.

LUCIFER
Since you once stood before my throne
and saw the consequences of my deeds,
you now have power to perceive me here.
I only hold dominion over souls
as long as they cannot behold me.
So I am forced now to release you.
Your seeking then may yield to you much fruit.
But those forbidden urges in your soul,
which prompted you to come here, *I* created
– forces that, stirring deep within your heart,
can open up to you this place's gates.
So in the end, you'll still rely on me.

CAPSTONE
My trust is not in you, but in the Lord.
You must withdraw. – – –

LUCIFER (*to audience*)
I find no access here into his soul.

I must depart from him and from this place
where he now seeks to trespass consciously.
So I must search for other means.
I cannot cross into this realm myself:
no God can enter here. But human souls
have never stayed awake there: If he enters,
the sultry heat will be to much for him.
In that hot darkness, spirit-wish is born.
He'll long to flee the confines of his body
and open portals of his soul to me.
(*to Capstone*)
I will depart, but never cease to fight.

CAPSTONE
And fighting, you will serve the plan of God.

(*Lucifer exits.*)

(*Capstone steps farther in*)

It's growing darker now.
Where am I? There are many places
in heav'n and in hell I'd recognize. But this
is wholly unfamiliar to my soul.
Heat surges all around me and
beckoning voices echo from the deep.

GREEN DEMONS (*whispering seductively from the darkness*)
In your feeling, hatred gnaws.
In your thinking, doubting sucks.
In your will, destruction reigns.
Come, come – give in to deep longing.
Sleep, sleep – and feel what is calling
Hate and feel good.
Destroy what hurts you.
Pain becomes pleasure; joy becomes pain.

CAPSTONE
Strange demons rise up from my body,
which seems to me a narrow stifling dungeon,
cruelly enclosing me in flaming urges.

I am surrounded by the forces I've
avoided and have always fought against.
They draw me down. The darkness overwhelms me.
And so my soul is thirsting for a moment
that will at last release me from the body.
Oh, who can hear me? My Lord God, where are you?
Why am I all alone within this place?

(*Troy appears*)

TROY
Michael. I am here.
You have come here with me on spirit wings.

CAPSTONE
Oh, Troy. I don't know where I am. I'm lost.
The air is stifling and I cannot think.

TROY
I know. This is an unfamiliar place to you.
But I am here. And with my heart I'll find the way.
So give your soul to all the pure delights of my
existence and our souls can find each other here.

CAPSTONE
What are these voices, whispering like demons?

TROY
They live here. They hold secrets. Let them be.

DEMONS
In your feeling, hatred gnaws.
In your thinking, doubting sucks.
In your will, destruction reigns.
Come, come – give in to deep longing.
Sleep, sleep – and feel what is calling
Hate and feel good.
Destroy what hurts you.
Pain becomes pleasure; joy becomes pain.

CAPSTONE
Oh, they seem dangerous. They speak of hatred,
destruction. And they're beckoning to me.

TROY
This is a place where green and jealous demons
defend their secrets in the cov'r of darkness.
If you will feel the strength'ning warmth
of all the joy and pleasure we have shared
and offer up this warmth to light-filled love,
then riddles human beings are wrestling with
can be unveiled to us within this trembling light;
the strength in us will grow to greatest heights;
and all the beings of this realm will surely
become illumined by majestic beauty.

CAPSTONE
Is this the right way then,
to satisfy my longing?
I'm seeking to unite my depths of soul
with my whole being.
Will I receive within myself
the penalty for my own error?
Am I consumed with passion or with love?

(*Marcus appears, dressed in shimmering light.*)

MARCUS
Love conquers passion when light illumines it.

TROY
Marcus!

MARCUS
      Troy.

CAPSTONE
      I knew you two would find each other.

MARCUS
We can shed light within this realm.
Without this human deed,
eternal darkness would hold sway.
Primordial powers born of light proclaim:
"Unlock the riddles from these demons' grasp."

DEMONS
What is this?
What strange god appears here in our realm?

MARCUS
No god can come here. Only human souls.

DEMONS
But a god has spoken through you.
Yes, it stinks. A goddess smell.
You were once her mediator!

MARCUS
I am a human being. Yet
from higher powers born of light,
I can proclaim the riddles of this place
unto my friends. – – Awake!
We can entice the riddles from the demons,
offer their secrets to the waiting gods,
and bring what's dark into the light.

DEMONS
Do not listen to him.
Sleep. He speaks delusion.
Darkness reigns here.
Do not shine your light here.
Go away. It burns me.
Tortures me.

MARCUS
Now your eternal darkness must give way.
Illumined by the light of gods

and love of worlds, you will become
new beings and this place will vanish.

DEMONS
No. We spit. We hate. Destroy.
Long ordained from ancient time,
we demand our realm, our might.
Out of here. You must retreat.

MARCUS
Do not be afraid. This is not your defeat.
Through light you will transform.
And all that you have guarded here so faithfully
will now be known and serve the gods.

DEMONS
No. We spit. We hate. Destroy.
Long ordained from ancient time,
we demand our realm, our might.
Out of here. You must retreat.

(*Barbara and Robert Finn appear*)

ROBERT
Let us bring light into this warming darkness,
for I'll tell stories to the child we hope for,
within our home. Here too, as we invite
this human soul into an earthly body,
a fairytale longs to shed some light,
a story of primeval origins
and turning points of time when fatherground
is planting seeds within the womb of worlds.

CAPSTONE
Oh! Who is this now entering this realm?
It seems that this young couple does not see us,
and yet their light shines softly all around them,
flickering warmly in the darkness.

DEMONS
(*Nearer to Robert and Barbara*)
One light only is allowed
here to tremble in our realm:
This one that springs up for couples,
seeking to create a child,
who arouse hot, burning forces,
from the sleep of man and woman.

TROY
What do you know about the bonds of love?
(*The Other Philia appears*)
– the riddles of the senses and their craving?
– the heav'nly meaning of the earthly body?

DEMONS
They are reaching for our secrets
of the flesh and of the blood
coursing through their hearts and veins,
heaving in their flesh and sinews;
urges, passions and desires
wildly surging here below;
churning and consuming flesh,
drinking with eternal thirst.

THE OTHER PHILIA
They baffle the senses
with hunger unceasing.
But what do they know
of the myst'ries of love?
The meal of communion's
a riddle to those
who never have tasted
the bread and the wine.

BARBARA
I know that, in the secret ways of nature,
green plants sprout into life and grow from pure
life forces, tended by the sprites of earth.

In us destructive demons can create.
New Light springs forth when human beings love.

THE OTHER PHILIA
And blissfully swimming
in heavenly blood,
this couple now knows
of the secrets of love.
And they feel the unquench-
able, undying thirst
as they eat of the bread
and they drink of the wine.

DEMONS
What is this? These souls awake?
Sleeping, they should be unconscious
of what happens here.
This cannot be.

MARCUS
Receive the light that they are sharing here,
reveal to us the secrets you conceal.
Be partners with us in the quest for life
and you will also meet the gods.

DEMONS
Light is burning, searing – torment.
Meet gods, you say?
But, no god has ever entered here.
This place is not for them.

TROY
Yet we are here and we, as human beings,
can also take our place among the gods.
A wealth of color will glisten everywhere,
and light will glimmer from the forms
surrounding us, and happiness of all
these beings flood the air with tones of joy.

DEMONS
You are reaching for our secrets
of the flesh and of the blood
coursing through your hearts and veins,
heaving in your flesh and sinews;
urges, passions and desires
wildly surging here below;
churning and consuming flesh,
drinking with eternal thirst.

(*Meaghan appears*)

CAPSTONE
Oh, Meaghan, you are here within these depths!
Can you appear now in your own true being?

MARCUS
She met me in the cosmic heights,
at revelation's very threshold,
where thoughts can follow threads that weave
through many destinies and earthly lives.
Although we have not met in sense existence,
I know her soul's path is akin to mine
in spiritual affinity through time, and
that something I had lost imbues her soul.
Her spirit seeks to speak to you and Troy,
and so she can appear now here with me.

DEMONS
What is this?
Now a god appears *indeed* here.
We can smell it.
You're illumined by a goddess!

MARCUS
Now she may enter here, for human beings
have joyfully invited her to come.

MEAGHAN
As if awakening within a dream,
my inner core could see that it is bound
up in a knot with many other souls
in threads that weave through other lives on earth.
And by the power of those fateful threads,
I have been drawn to you now here in thought,
as Troy has called you to this gloomy place
where love and hate do battle for our souls.

CAPSTONE
I have seen many strange and wondrous things
upon the journey that has brought me here,
but never would have thought that, Meaghan, you
would find your way into this realm of demons.

MEAGHAN
It was the hardest testing of your soul
when I was summoned from my body.
You told me of your love for Troy Fels
and of the wisdom that you hear through me.
And as you spoke, the purest light of wisdom
within an instant flooded through my heart
and it transformed all sorrow into blissful joy.
Only one heavenly thought lived in me:
you gave me faith, yes faith in Him who gave
himself in sacrifice for all mankind,
who gave his body and his blood for all.
This thought had power to give my soul new wings
that carried me to revelation's threshold
and to this soul who's led me here to you.

DEMONS
Curse him, curse him! He has robbed you,
broken bonds of blood and marriage,
taken what was yours and killed it,
shattered rules that ward off chaos.
Hatred's fire, wild and burning
must destroy him now and always.

MEAGHAN
But nothing has been taken that was mine.
No jealousy or condemnation can
reside within the midst of such abundance.
And why is it assumed that I would judge?
Has someone issued a complaint? Not I.
Long have I been aware now, Michael, that
a dreaming youthful shadow of your self
was hidden and estranged from you. I've prayed
that you would reunite yourself with it,
but knew you had to find it for yourself.
And I rejoice that you can now regard
your earthly body with desire and longing,
and that the wish can rise within your soul
for gravity of earth to draw you down
into your body's sheath where you can feel
and hold the sense of joy in warmth of life,
for you have long avoided this. If what
I say is sacrilege, may God set me straight.
You are transcending laws of nature and
the customary ways that ward off chaos.
You lead the way in times when, freed from dogma
we each must use our powers of thought in freedom,
perceiving for ourselves what's right and good.
And if your soul is clouded by desires,
you'll find your way to your true path in Christ.
You still are welcome at His Holy Supper.
For who can guess the body's heavenly meaning?
Who can begin to understand the blood?
The body bears within itself the means
to recreate on earth what is divine.

MARCUS
Life's hidden secrets are revealed when
love penetrates with light all earth existence
and can awaken in our human souls
the heavenly meaning of the blood and body
as an eternal, sacred riddle that
our earthly senses cannot solve.

CAPSTONE
The radiant light of thinking penetrates
this hidden region and illumines it.
I now begin to know the demons' secrets.
Their riddles can be lifted up to God.

THE OTHER PHILIA
And you who abstained
have now tasted but once
at the table of longing
that never is bare.
The breath of your life
you have drawn from those lips
that are warm and belovéd.
The holiest glowing
has melted your heart
into tremulous waves,
and you've lifted your eyes
and, measuring boundless
expanses of heaven,
you'll eat of the body
and drink of the blood
in eternal devotion
to Him who has Risen.

MARCUS
So through the body we can serve the Spirit;
and the true meaning of our life of soul
can only show itself when in our body
the strength of the 'I Am' confirms itself.

(*Silence.*)

DEMONS (*quietly*)
When you speak like this,
my tongue falls silent.

MARCUS
We honor you. Your riddles will live on.
The powers you've wielded here will not be lost.
In light they will increase and fructify.

DEMONS
Now *you* speak riddles.
And we can only wait.
What is to come, we do not know.

ROBERT FINN
Long, long ago, in primeval ages of the earth,
the gods cast metals out of the heavens
down into the depths of earth.
When human beings had developed skills
to craft these metals with their hands and tools,
they smoothed the walls and rounded pillars of
an underground rock chamber near a river,
then molded figures of three kings –
of gold, of silver and of bronze.
A fourth and motley king,
of all three metals mixed,
was ugly and misshapen,
hunched over his giant club.
The bronze king held a sword for strength and courage,
the silver king a scepter full of beauty;
the king of gold received a crown of oak leaves
for his wisdom.
Long ages passed.
Green creatures living underground,
crawling and slith'ring in the dark,
explored by touch the shapes they found:
the columns, walls and figures.
And now and then a man would come
through rocky passageways,
an old man with a lamp,
into the dark and secret chamber of the kings.
At last, a time came when the gods
called upon the gold king to perform

a special task.
For a new era soon was to begin
when human beings would attain
abilities in wisdom, beauty, strength and love.
But at such time of dawning powers,
a god must first imbue some single person
on the earth.
So now it was the Gold King's task,
through vision and his wisdom,
to look o'er all the earth and choose
the one to be the vessel for a goddess
who now would manifest in earthly life.
The Gold King looked throughout the land,
below the ground,
over the earth and waters and
on both sides of the large and flowing river.
His gaze fell on a beautiful Princess, Lily,
tending her garden on the other side
of this great river. She was chosen.
From that day on, whatever living thing
the Princess touched would die.
For this new higher life in her must bring
all lower life to death.
People and pets died at her touch.
She grieved each one of them.
And so she longed to find the cause of this distress.
She crossed the river with the ferryman
to visit the wise old man
who took her through dark passageways,
into the rocky chamber of the kings.
They groped in darkness, for the old man's lamp,
he said, must not illumine what is dark,
but only shine where there's already light.
The Lily touched the four kings one by one
and each one came to life.
For though her touch now killed all living things,
it had the pow-er to bring stone to life.
And when the Gold King came to life, she asked,
"Why must I bring such suffering and death

on all the friends and creatures whom I love?"
The Gold King spoke:
He told of her divinely chosen role.
"When will this suff'ring end?" the Lily asked.
"When within the span of one day's time,"
the Gold King then replied,
"you hear the words thrice spoken,
'The time is now at hand,'
you will then know
that soon your joy will be fulfilled:
Greatest misfortune you can then regard
as greatest joy.
For this rock temple will arise and stand
beside the river,
near your garden on the other side,
and a great bridge will then be built
to span the river
for crowds of people, vehicles and animals
to pass with ease across and back.
Until that day when this shall be fulfilled,
whatever living thing you touch will die,
and anyone who meets your gaze
will lose his spirit."
The Princess then returned unto her garden,
knowing that she must never touch a friend or animal
or ever cast her gaze on anyone.

(End of scene)

18) Born Again

*(The office of The Bridge of Christ, and the home of Michael Capstone
and Meaghan Gerald. The sun is shining brightly through the window.
Michael is sitting, coming out of his meditation begun in scene 13.
Meaghan is still lying on the couch, covered with the warm
blanket. She stirs, awakens, rises as from a long refreshing sleep.
Later, Stratham – as a thought-form of Capstone – Astrid, Philia, the
Other Philia and Luna appear.)*

MEAGHAN
A thought had power to give my soul new wings.
"But nothing has been taken that was mine.
The body bears within itself the means
to re-create on earth what is divine."
These words I spoke within a realm of demons,
and they re-echo still within my soul.
The Holy Spirit has laid hold on me,
and certainty of many other lives
awakens me from spirit sleep.
I now can grasp my part within the knot
that's woven by the threads of destiny.
(She looks at Capstone.)
I'll leave him to his quiet contemplation,
for he has now withstood his greatest trial.
(She picks up Celia Gottlieb's book and exits.)

CAPSTONE *(Alone)*
(to himself)
I am alive to what I've done,
aware of what I've seen.
Renewed, I am reborn to being.
Yes, born again,
my soul's empowered with vision
by God's embracing, noble spirit light.
Now, if I fail to perceive the tasks of life
and to rework the life that I've been dreaming,
I know that I will be forever bound
to empty nothingness.

In quiet contemplation,
a picture rose before my soul. I saw
the battles I had struggled through in spirit,
before my birth, in order to create
this life out of a former life.
And, uninvolved, I could pass calmly through
these storms and battles
to see, in image and tableaux,
the actions and the deeds of former days.
Without emotion, I beheld a time
not long ago when, by a fellowship of friends,
a temple had been built, which later burned.
Meaghan was there, but as a man.
Troy's sister, also as a man,
worked with me as an artist to create
the temple's forms and images.
And Troy, as a woman, was a nurse
and very close to me. – –
And many others whom I do not know
in *this* life. – Troy's father also
was there, but died while he was young.

(*Stratham/Strader becomes visible.*)

I feel my soul was closely linked with his.
And even now, he vividly approaches
as spirit image on my soul's horizon.

ASTRID
(*At some distance, still in chains, though somewhat freer here.*)
You are indebted to this man
from deeds wrought in an ancient temple.
His soul did not ask for redress
in your last earthly life,
but now that ancient debt can be repaid.
Through powers of thought his image gave to you
in the far distant spheres of Sun,
you now can recognize him here on earth,
since he, within your present life, fulfills
the picture that his soul had shown you then.

PHILIA

The meaning of life's course on earth is now
revealed for you within your own soul sheaths,
through roots of thought that were implanted by
an image of this soul akin to yours,
in Saturn's many-colored rays of light
within your cosmic midnight hour.

THE OTHER PHILIA

The image could indeed move closer still,
but could not pierce the sphere of your own life.
Its urge toward your existence you held back,
so you could find yourself again on earth
before it flowed into your inmost being.

LUNA

The picture that you still behold, so far
out on the shoreline of your soul-sphere
can move now ever closer unto you.
Before that life, this fire-soul was revealed
on the horizon of your spirit sight.
You filled a former life with powers of grace
endowed by a still earlier life.
And thus a life in ancient times long past,
which had flowed by in solemn growth
and planted seeds of solitude, shed light
on one you lived made dark by selfish craving.
Knowledge of *that* life was too much to bear.
You fled to realms of cosmic light and learned
that what seems evil may be changed to good
if some good being offers it its guidance.

CAPSTONE

I feel myself knowingly strengthened by wisdom.
"You shall know the Truth, and the Truth shall set you free."

(End of scene)

19) Rock of Ages

(Simon Stratham alone in meditation. Ahriman appears, Astrid at his side in chains.)

STRATHAM
I have been conscious of you in your own domain
and pitied you in your eternal suffering.
Now here on earth, I know I lack the soul force
needed to meet you as you must be met,
which I have granted you as a deposit
for what my daughter has attained through you.
But in her wrestling soul she'll gain the power
to recognize you in your true reality.
The soul force you hold captive, will regain
her rightful place and work and weave in her
full power in harmony with all her sisters.
Till then, through love and strength of my dear Celia,
I have the clarity to face you here.

AHRIMAN
Whether Joanna yet will recognize
and stand against me we shall see. –
Yet you yourself are still indebted to me.
From whom have you gained knowledge for your work?
In what realm have you found the clarity
that's led you to your great accomplishment?
You cannot now deny: all came from me.
I gladly helped you stage by stage as you
developed plans, according to the laws
of measure and of number,
through which you thought to serve the human being.
In your last life, I could defeat your work
and your ridiculous machine,
through criticism by a clever man
and by your early death.
Though ancient cosmic law denies me access
to read your book of life a second time,
your children are not so protected.

I still can read what's written in the book of fate
about your stepson's course of life.
I'd hoped that he'd give Lucifer some joy,
but now he's interfering with my plans.
He knows too much. And he can think
too independently. $-$ $-$
And what about this clever new technique,
by which you mean to help and free mankind
in every walk of life: Although its nature in itself
is good and can bring good results
for human beings, you do not see that,
under the influence of Brother Lucifer,
people will use your methodology
to capture what they want, become complacent
and rid themselves of guilt and of anxiety.
It all depends upon the one from whom
the work has flowed. And that is me. Not you.

STRATHAM
You are the master of deceit and speak in lies,
but only fools would try to slink past you,
and cowardly avoid error's source;
you sometimes speak the truth. $-$ $-$
One question I will ask you. Can you see
into the realms that stand between
you and your brother Lucifer?

AHRIMAN
There is no realm where beings live
who would be hostile to my need for entrance.

STRATHAM
Then listen well.
You may indeed have access to my work.
And it may seem to you I lack the force
within my soul to keep it from you. But
friendship and love are never visible to you.
You cannot see their kind, redeeming force.
And what a human soul may lack,

through long and winding paths of destiny,
can be made whole when others join with him.

(*Michael Capstone appears in spirit.*)

For harmony of spirits can achieve
what each alone could never bring about.
This has unwavering force in spirit realms.
And my eternal being, which I owe
to other realms and beings than your own,
will always offer to humanity
this work that freely flows
from forces that you cannot comprehend.

AHRIMAN
I mean to fight.
Your stepson Troy's time is up.
It's finished.
Mario Troy Fels, that faithful rock,
is no more. He'll die tonight.
It will appear to be an accident.
And who's to say?
My work is often called an accident on earth.
I work in chaos.

(*Ahriman exits. Beat.*)

CAPSTONE
In silence I will speak the Word I owe to you,
held back within an ancient holy rite.
For what seems evil may be changed to good
if some good being offers it its guidance.
Love treasures all and asks not whence it comes
but how to use what rises into life
from world depths, however it springs forth.

STRATHAM
A hopeful word of friendship echoes here
sounding mysteriously from ancient times.
This word draws forth the purest love of worlds.

As from a long lost friend, it sounds but gently.
It whispers near and yet I cannot grasp it.
What works and weaves between us through this Word?

CAPSTONE
Enkindle in yourself a fire, to burn
away the error woven by your selfhood.
Burn up yourself as well, along with error's fabric.
Seek your own flame within the cosmic fire.
Unite yourself with Cosmic Self,
and it will grant to you existence.
In burning, you will gain your own true being.

STRATHAM
As if they echoed long-past sacred rites
these words resound from wellsprings of my being.
And through them I feel deeply how much I
am needful of that god who radiates
His highest healing power only when
He Himself dwells within our inmost soul
and Who, in death, proclaims life lovingly.

(*End of scene*)

20) Bitter Ashes

(The Temple Monument. Marcus alone in meditation. Stella Sophia as spirit only and later Troy.)

MARCUS
A star of soul – there – at the spirit shore. –
It's drawing nearer, close in spirit brightness –
approaching as a spirit form.
Active and alive – it comes to me:
it is myself in former times. I see . . .

(Stella Sophia appears behind him.)

a woman with an orphan child
to whom she gives a mother's love.
She seeks advice from her beloved teacher.
I know this story. I have often heard
and read accounts of Benedictus' pupil
Maria. Could it be that I was she?

STELLA SOPHIA
I was that child you raised so faithfully.
To womanhood I grew and when the temple burned
and all seemed lost, I brought your teacher's work
to a new land, and there it flourished.
When you again took on a body's sheath –
when you were but a child – we met again,
my dear Marcus. And I could then return to you
the motherly love you once gave me.

MARCUS
How can that be? That I've returned so quickly.

STELLA SOPHIA
You know that this is not the usual way,
but at this turning point in time
when so much is at stake,
it's possible for groups of human beings to
return to earth quite soon to carry on
an uncompleted task.

MARCUS
Oh, how am I to understand this riddle?
For everyone who speaks about Maria
tells of her powers of sacrifice, clear thinking,
her selfless and devoted heart, her strong
and fearless loving will and seership.
I've given all my strength and my devotion
preserving Benedictus' work, which she embodied,
but I do not have her capacities.

STELLA SOPHIA
Gaze further into what you have experienced.
In the clear weaving of your own true seeing,
the answer will appear to you.

MARCUS
I see it now. I look upon that life,
behold my deeds, the words I spoke that tore
our fellowship asunder. O horrible.
I feel the weight of this self-knowledge.

SOPHIA
"Many a human being walks the earth
who would behold with bitter shame
how little in his present life there is
that corresponds to what he did before."

MARCUS
Again, these words strike deep within my soul.
I spoke them once myself and now as
self-knowledge they return to me.
I see − − −
When Benedictus died and left his body,
the godly being left Maria too,
that being who illumined her till then.
The Prince of Darkness
entered the body's sheath,
attempting to destroy through me
the work of Benedictus and his pupils.

STELLA SOPHIA
And yet, through opposition's force, that power
of darkness can promote the plan of wisdom,
which would convert the evil into good.
So comprehend now that your being had
to change into its opposite. Because
good spirits spoke so often through your lips,
world karma did not spare your friends from also
hearing through them the prince of hell.

MARCUS
How terrible. – –
And yet I have the strength to bear it.
I know now what I did and who I was.
How can I reconcile it with who
I am today and find my further tasks?

SOPHIA
Know, in the heart that in Maria lived,
discipleship of spirit had enkindled
forces enabling her to keep self-love
apart forever from all knowledge.

MARCUS
Her holy solemn vow – does not belong to me.
Where can I find the strength to make that vow?

STELLA SOPHIA
What powers you have now, truly are your own.
A godly being of human wisdom
once worked through you and now can manifest
through many people:
The way has been prepared through you.
(*she disappears*)

MARCUS
Oh, Troy, you knew it, didn't you?
You would have told me my soul lived once as

Maria, Benedictus' closest pupil,
but I never asked you.
I had to see it for myself.
(*Troy enters. He is carrying an urn.*)
(*beat*)

TROY
I've brought you Stella Sophia's ashes.

(*End of scene*)
(*End of Act VI*)

Act Seven

21) Ashes to Ashes (*continued*)

(The Temple Monument. Marcus and Troy. The same moment as at the close of the previous scene. Stella Sophia is gone. Troy is holding the urn.)

TROY
I've brought you Stella Sophia's ashes.

MARCUS
Troy. . . . Are you here?

TROY
The question demands a yes.

MARCUS
I thought that you were in America.

TROY
I am with you. And I have brought her ashes.

MARCUS
Take them back.

TROY
This is the right place for them.
The origin of all her work was here.
This monument to our lost Temple
can also hold the memory of her.
But I fear for you, because you are my friend.
Come away from here.

MARCUS
This is the right place for me.
This is where Benedictus consecrated
the Temple on the earth,
the spiritual school of Micha-él
made manifest and visible.

TROY
The Temple that you seek does not exist.
Not here. It is no longer only here.

MARCUS
This is the place where Benedictus gave
his pupils mantras and the task
of recognizing their own mutual karma,
of bringing it into harmony,
and moving it into earthly work.
It's esoteric heart has to be here.

TROY
Wherever people truly meet in spirit,
and find themselves in one another,
uniting Light and Love;
when human deeds of blessing
join with the aims of gods,
the Temple will be manifest
as truth of spirit shines through warmth of soul.

MARCUS (*playing along, ironically*)
On a plane, on the street, in a cafe . . .

TROY
Yes.

MARCUS
I know that people say that;
I've heard it many times.
But often it can really be illusion.
A ploy by Lucifer,
distracting from reality.

TROY
Then let it die as an illusion.
And make it live as a reality.
Work together with the Sophia community

and also with my new church friends.
Make sure that the connection is sustained.
The thread from ancient mystery places, through
the Temple that once stood upon this ground.
Hold that thread into the future.
You, only you now on the earth can see
the bridge. The time has come.
The Temple that once stood here
is turning inside out.
It's op'ning up for everyone who seeks it.
For all humanity.

MARCUS
But it was here that the foundation stone
was laid for the new mysteries.

TROY
It lives within your heart,
wherever you may be. And it will grow
wherever you work with others. You don't need
to stay here.

MARCUS
Who will maintain this place in these dark times?

TROY
I know the people working here.
They can and will maintain all this without you,
the books, this monument, the archives;
the monumental hall as an active meeting place,
one of many such places around the world.
The times are turning and this archive's task
is also changing.
Some places on the earth are called
by cosmic destiny
to sacred work for periods of time,
and it will give them other tasks when,
in this service, they exhaust their strength.

MARCUS
This temple's destiny's not yet fulfilled.

TROY
It faced its own probation when in
a cosmic moment fraught with destiny,
the error of one woman
had to crack open this seed's shell
to fructify the spirit life of all
humanity through pain.
You sacrificed your light, so that new light
could then be born in darkness
for all humanity.

MARCUS
Through all the work that Benedictus left us,
the threads that karma spins in world becoming
must be woven into spirit working
on the earth, here where the Temple stood.

TROY
Why do you seek the living among the dead?
It is not here.   –   –

(*Still holding the urn, he blows on it. It turns to dust. Troy disappears in the cloud of dust. Marcus is left alone.*)

(*End of scene*)

22) Sacrifice

(Finns' house. Barbara, Robert, Capstone and, later, Joanna. Barbara is visibly pregnant. Somber but peaceful atmosphere. Some time has passed since Troy died.)

BARBARA
You're welcome here.
You're Troy's friend.
So you are our friend too.

ROBERT
It's good of you to come.
Troy's death has been a shock to all of us.
You saw him just before the accident.

CAPSTONE
Yes. Only days before.
I know he would have wanted me to come here.
He wanted to create a kind of bridge
between our two communities. And now
I've seen that we have much in common from
our former lives on earth, and we may also,
together, find a way to serve the future.

ROBERT
You are a very different man
from him we heard about in news reports.

CAPSTONE
The man I was would not have spoken in this way.

BARBARA
What paths of soul have led to such a change?

CAPSTONE
I've been allowed to see within myself
the fruits that ripen when a soul can enter
the spirit realm at the appointed time.
God's spirit light now shines on everything

and quickens conscious forces in my soul
that can enhance clear-minded thoughtfulness
and guide me everywhere I go.
At every step that I now take in life
I know I may fulfill the obligations
that grow out of my former lives on earth.
My plan of destiny has granted me
a peaceful joy that comes with forces
that can shape my deeds in life
through knowledge of myself.

BARBARA
Our home is blessed to host you and to hear
these words so humbly spoken.

CAPSTONE
Although I've never met you in this life,
I feel that I can speak to you as if
I were in quiet solitude or speaking
alone with Troy. With any other people,
I don't think I'd be able
to bring such words across my lips.
But here with you I speak with ease.

ROBERT
And is your church still active in its work?

CAPSTONE
Our church has now been banned by the Authorities.
I understand that your community
still has considerable autonomy.

BARBARA
Yes, some. Joanna's using her connections
to help us to continue some of our activities.
We now can share raw milk from our own cows
within our own community.
Who knows! If she could get to know you better,
perhaps she also would be able to help you.

CAPSTONE
I can't expect that she will work with me
or be of any service to our cause.
But now she is our only hope.
Although I know the likelihood is small,
I have to ask her for her help.

ROBERT
Perhaps she'll want to speak with you.
She knows you're here.
She came here yesterday,
still mourning for her brother.
She has been wandering
around the house and garden deep in thought –
as if she's pondering some great decision.
Her duties with the Cultural Authority
are trying on her soul, and they demand
a lot of strength.

BARBARA
And yet she's always said that she's determined
to change the policies and regulations
to allow for and support the practices
that flow out of our spirit teaching.

CAPSTONE
I don't believe that it is possible –
and certainly it's not ideal –
to merge the spiritual life into
the sphere of politics and rights.
And yet I must admit
that, in these troubled times,
we have to face reality.

JOANNA (*enters, speaking as if to herself, only half aware of the others in the room*)
I was shocked and bewildered when my brother died.
Was it an accident?
Was it a stroke of destiny?

He died so suddenly.
He's with me constantly in spirit,
his radiant, uncompromising quest;
his doubts about our world government.
I no longer know what I would say to him.
He gave his life.
I was too late to save the church from closing;
there was nothing I could do;
I changed my mind too late.
And how could I convince my officers
and colleagues that the church should be
allowed now to continue after all?
(*Seeing Capstone*)
Oh. Michael Capstone. – –
I have been thinking about you.
I know this may sound strange to you, but I
now feel I can speak openly. I have to.
I've had an inkling for some time
of how my individuality appeared
within a certain circle of spirit pupils
in a not-too-distant life on earth.
But, in a kind of waking dream,
I now could see it for myself. I was a man.
Marcus was there; he was a woman and
dear friend. And both of *you*
(*Barbara and Robert*). My father also as
a younger man; and you (*Capstone*) were there, but older.
And I worked closely with you:
We built a Temple.
We stood together, all of us,
and took a bold new step in spirit work.
But dark and adversarial forces crushed our hopes
and violent disagreement broke our fellowship.
Ever since I confronted you in your church that day,
I have felt stunned and empty.
My understanding of the world was shaken.
I'm overcome by doubts.
I feel that thoughts are growing old and stale.
I once had opened up my heart

to a true knowledge of the spirit.
But now that the ideas that I've worked out
within myself stream forth to humankind,
I fear the consequences of my work.
One thought alone
forms the inner ground for me to stand on,
the words you quoted from the Bible.

CAPSTONE
Paul's letter to Galatians.

JOANNA
"Not I, but Christ lives in me." – –
I was misguided in my opposition
to your church, – –
I now can see how wrong I was
to work for its destruction.

CAPSTONE
I know we have had much to disagree about,
but we can find a way to work together.
I know the vast majority of people
are blindly following the regulations
and that there will be penalties and dangers
for defying them.
We now know that we may
even have to risk our lives.
But I believe we have to try.
At least I know that I do.
And I invite you now to join me.
I offer what I can to help support
and to sustain your school and farm
in any way that's possible.
Even if it has to be in secret.
We'll find a way. I'm asking you to help.

JOANNA
I can no longer work in this regime.
Its opposition to your church

and many of its tactics
are now intolerable to me.
I have decided to resign tomorrow morning.

CAPSTONE
What will you do? Go back to university?

JOANNA
Most likely not.
I would be banned from all my work
in public and in academic life.
The Cultural Authority would say that I
no longer support their ideology.

ROBERT
Do you?   (*Ahriman appears, listening.*)

JOANNA
I know it also has a kernel of the truth.
It is the wisdom of the current *policies* I question.

CAPSTONE
If you were still prepared to work to change
or circumvent those policies, I would be too.
Working within the world administration,
you could perhaps ensure
that something of our work
and our initiatives can still survive.

JOANNA
(*Slight pause*) All right. I will continue
to work with the Authority,
and do my best to
allow our work and yours to still continue . . . .

(*Ahriman exits.*)

I have to trust now in the guidance of the spirit . . . .
that, even with our differences –
and perhaps also because of them –
we all can work together for the good.

BARBARA (*to Capstone*)
It seems unthinkable
that Troy is not here with us.
Since he's the one who led you here to us.

ROBERT
I think that in a story
I could express what we are feeling here
about our dear friend Troy.

JOANNA
Please do. My empty soul is thirsty for
the nourishment your stories bring.

CAPSTONE
Yes, do tell us one of your tales. Troy told
me many times about their healing power.

ROBERT
The gods once made a being out of love.
She was so powerful and radiant
and warm that they divided her in two.
And each of these two halves of love
then longed throughout long ages of the earth
to one day reunite themselves again,
as one of them, the warmth of love,
was cast down –
to live beneath the surface of the earth,
to slither through the rocky passageways –
a snake whose body was all green.
Her other half, the light of love,
became a beautiful Lily,
living in a palace as a princess,
near a great river.
And on the other side of this great river,
beneath the surface of the earth, there was
an underground chamber, carved from stone.
There the green snake often slithered in the dark,
discovering shapes and figures in this rock chamber –

statues of kings carved of precious metals:
gold, silver and bronze.
According to an ancient prophesy,
this temple was to rise one day
and stand beside the river.
A bridge, spanning the river,
would also then be built
for crowds of people, vehicles and animals
to cross in both directions.
One night, in the middle of the night,
the green snake slithered once again
into the rocky chamber.
But this time, she shone with a glowing light
that she had never shown before.
She could see now
what had remained hidden to her sight,
revealed only to her sense of touch.
The kings then spoke
and she conversed with them
of gold and of light and of speech.
An old man then stepped through the rock walls
into the stone chamber.
He carried a shining lamp.
The kings now asked him questions,
which he answered.
The words he spoke
then echoed through the temple rock:
"The time's at hand!"
With this the old man and the snake
disappeared again
into the stone passageways.

The next night, in the middle of the night,
the large heavy door of the rock chamber,
which had always remained
sealed with a golden lock,
suddenly burst open
and a whole procession
of people and creatures entered:

a prince, the princess, the old man and
his wife, two will-o-wisps,
a pug dog, a canary and a hawk.
But the green snake was nowhere to be seen.
For the third time the old man
spoke the words of the prophecy.
The rock temple moved through the earth,
under the river and up on the other side.
Throngs of travelers crossed a wide bridge
that had mysteriously appeared.
The green snake had transformed
into thousands of precious stones,
which then became the great bridge
that had been foretold by the prophecy,
and the Temple became
the most frequented upon the earth.

(*End of scene*)

23) Umstülpung

(A few years later. The offices of Gumption-Truegood, a business run by the former church board members. Meaghan and Celia are in the midst of their work together. Later, Blythe Truegood, Thea Twist, George Battle and Raymond Gumption appear above in an adjacent meeting room upstairs.)

CELIA
And our friends in the Northwest island
community send you their thanks and greetings.
They express their ever growing trust
and confidence in your support and colleagueship.
In their remote and hidden chapel they're already
holding the ritual secretly themselves,
thanks to your guidance and advice.

MEAGHAN
So, even though we have no church,
they, and many others too,
are sharing in our work
with warm enthusiasm, and
always the same reasons,
because of real experience of the spirit.

CELIA
They say that they made contact with us just in time,
that all their old traditions had grown stale
and superficial, lacking the support
of direct knowledge and experience.
I hear the same continually
in every place I visit on my travels.
New interest is growing among people
who are not satisfied with the official views,
but seek relationship
to the divine in freedom.
And more and more have courage to defy
the World Authorities and hold their meetings.
Although there have been raids

by armed security patrols,
these small communities are now,
in secret, educating children based
upon their own creative will
and some have started farms and gardens
with help from messages that I've conveyed
from Barbara Finn, who's also learned
some useful practices from them.
They feel quite free in their relationship with us,
and share their wisdom and experience
and struggles. And they sense that, through
our open friendships, with each other and with them,
they can connect – by an unbroken thread –
to ancient sacred paths and also to
eternal aims of the angelic world.

MEAGHAN
We're very fortunate that you're still able
to travel freely and to carry messages
among so many places.

CELIA
With all my talk of angels, the authorities
regard me as a harmless and eccentric woman,
like those who lead so many souls
into illusion, far from any earthly work.
So I can also help my husband's correspondence
with the few physicists, psychologists
and scientists who have begun
collaborating with him. – They exchange
research on healing and technology. –
As long as the authorities believe
that we're promoting practices
and substances that will intoxicate
or mollify the population, –
my travel and our work are not forbidden.
And Robert Finn is also still allowed
to travel. Through his puppetry
and storytelling, which authorities

perceive as harmless drivel, he can share
his wife's experiences in agriculture
and in gardening and *his* in childhood education.
Many performing artists are inspired by his work.

MEAGHAN
And how is Bar-ba-ra and Robert's child?

CELIA
He's talking like a little waterfall.

MEAGHAN
And Michael tells me that your daughter –
in spite of government restrictions –
is seeking ways to share what spirit knowledge
can bring to agriculture and to education.

CELIA
I'm grateful that Joanna and your husband
have found a way to work together now
and overcome their differences,
so practical endeavors in
nutrition and in education
are not as thwarted as they might be if
Joanna were not working where she is.

MEAGHAN
It still seems strange to me your daughter now
supports our work, since she
so actively opposed it for so long
and she's still working for the Cultural
Authority, which seems to be our foe.

CELIA
Joanna can be full of contradictions.
She struggles in her soul to find the way
to rightly serve the future of humanity.
Her brother's death – three years ago now –
is still affecting her quite deeply.

MEAGHAN
Ah, yes. Your son's untimely death is still
affecting all of us quite deeply.
I'm grateful and in awe that God –
through Troy and the Angels –
has brought this group of individuals
together for the Spirit's work
in many different areas of life.
Now what about the medical endeavors?

CELIA
A group of nurses and physicians
who had known Troy have asked my husband
to help them to develop natural
and homeopathic medicines
and remedies. They're interested
in certain indications from the work
of Benedictus and his nurse,
Maria Treufels.
And writers interested in ancient literature
have asked that Marcus Lilly help them
in understanding how the ancient mysteries
can be interpreted for modern times.

MEAGHAN
I am surprised all this is possible
when travel and communication are so limited.

CELIA
It is miraculous, I know. But with
good will and with the help and guidance of
the angels, we are finding ways to meet
and to communicate without attracting
attention from investigators.

MEAGHAN
Indeed, my husband's also meeting with
historians and architects.

Our colleague Thea Twist and I
are helping people secretly renew
religious life and celebrate the festivals.
So much is happening that makes it clear how
our work is growing more and more
and how we're meeting all our obligations.
Although the vast majority of people have
no interest in what we are doing, those who *do*
are finding what they need for their own work
and lives and their relationships
with family, friends and colleagues.

CELIA
I often see our angels rejoicing all around us,
as we are carrying on our work. It seems to me
fulfilling and noble when people
can freely find their own devotional life
and come together without prescribed beliefs.
And look how work can be ennobled
when spiritually active human beings
take hold of it, − − −

(*Lights shift, revealing an adjacent meeting room above, Blythe
Truegood, Thea Twist, George Battle and Raymond Gumption mid-
meeting.*)

developing new products that supply
useful things for daily human needs,
which are truly beautiful.
Craftsmanship is combined with art to bring
good taste to ordinary life.
So that the soul bestows true meaning on
what otherwise is like a corpse.

MEAGHAN
Listen. Upstairs the board is meeting now.

THEA
Here are some more designs from Robert Finn
and other artists there in the Sophia

Community. I think these could fulfill
the needs our customers expressed to us.
Of course they don't fit government
requirements. Will we be able to
deliver them by secret courier?

GEORGE
Yes, that is working well enough for now.
I have been able to communicate with
Joanna Thomason again and she
is doing what she can to keep us out
of trouble with authorities, so we
can carry on providing faithful service
to all our customers.

RAYMOND
Now, who else could appreciate
what we produce and make good use
of all this work of ours?

BLYTHE
It's clear to me that all our work
can only grow and thrive if it
is met by a sufficient understanding
for ways of working based on knowledge
and experience of the spirit.

RAYMOND
That's why I am proposing we provide
financial backing and support
not only for the fields of work in which
our friends are now engaged. But also for
the schooling Simon Stratham has in mind,
where people speak about direct experience of
the living Christ and where our Michael Capstone,
as well as Celia Gottlieb, also
this Marcus Lilly who has come from Europe,
are able to present and foster
a knowledge of the spirit

among the people and communities
we are befriending and who show
some interest in our products.

GEORGE
I have a plan already for a way
to manage such a schooling
despite constraints:
Meaghan can work with Simon . . .
(*Lights shift back to Meaghan and Celia.*)

MEAGHAN
The interweaving of our different fields of work,
truly brings the power of our Lord
into practical deeds in all areas of life.
I have to say, your husband is
most capably co-or-di-nating this.

CELIA
Good fortune brought him to this work.
You and your colleagues recognized
the essence of his spirit.
Sensing his high human obligations,
you created a field of action for this man.

MEAGHAN
It's clearly evident in him how human thinking
can be productive when it has a sense
for what is real. He owes the
techniques that he's developed,
without a doubt, to intuition's light.
And from them countless blessings flow.
He has discovered forces that
were out of reach and made them real,
accessible to anyone.

CELIA
Your praise shows your ability to see
he has his place within this circle.

No outer hindrances can set themselves
against his spirit's aims.
We will continue to reveal and share
our path and our experience with others,
who then begin to feel the need
to permeate their life with spirit knowledge.

MEAGHAN
We cannot claim that we
have wiped out egotism, but
we strive to conquer it among ourselves.

CELIA
Even if what we're doing doesn't last
– *outwardly,*
or is destroyed by the authorities
or the whole world despises and
ridicules it, it will have stood once on the earth
as an example for humanity.
It will work on in spirit. This is what
the angels and our spirit knowledge teach us.

MEAGHAN
I'm dedicated to this work because
its ways and methods are quite clear to me.
I know that those who put their trust in us
aren't led astray, entangled in illusion;
their faculty to make their own decisions
remains intact. Clear judgment, common sense
and spirit knowledge and experience
are applied to daily work and serving others.

CELIA
Dear Meaghan. You appreciate
the situation and the dangers threat'ning us.
We simply could not do without you!
Your cooperation makes it possible
for us to work with angels and to serve
true spirit goals. Your good counsel

strengthens us, as I know you strengthened
your church for many years.

MEAGHAN
I think that I can safely say,
we truly render service to humanity.
This is no phantom of hot air,
no flight of fancy. Many places are now
secretly buzzing with activity:
This work is bearing fruit.

CELIA
If we continue to support each other
and work together, even in these troubled times,
the prospects do indeed seem good.
The angels are rejoicing and stand by us.
They are also telling me that
still harder times will come.

I will convey your messages to Simon,
and those from Blythe and Raymond too.
Please know you have his fullest confidence,
and that he's grateful for your management,
administrative work and your advice.
It's been a pleasure seeing you again.

MEAGHAN
So much is possible when we can find
the way to truly meet each other's souls.
For human beings can so often seem
like separate worlds apart, each one alone;
but when the gulf between us can be bridged,
great good may be created for the world.

(End of scene)

24) Circenses Post Panem

(The office of the Cultural Authority, same as Scene 2. Trauta S. Harris again sits on her seat of judgment. Joanna sits where Michael Capstone sat, Ahriman in the background listening.)

TRAUTA HARRIS
We've long embraced ideas
your book made popular.
And as advisor you've contributed
to forming and enforcing policies
and regulations. It has also not
escaped from our awareness that you
are helping certain groups to circumvent
some of the rules and guidelines.
Your friend Marcus Lilly who
I understand is now in North America,
has influence and access
in an archival cult'ral center
in the middle of Europe.
The task now falls to me to ask that you
advise – that is, to offer you the opportunity
to open up to all the people of the world
the knowledge and the work
that until now was kept within
your close community –
to work with us to form
a union of all cultures.
Thus you and he can help to bring,
through government authority,
what's needed by the soul, once
repletion and relief from hunger are achieved.

JOANNA
I have long sought for ways
to join our earthly work,
with world leadership
uniting all humanity.

I will now resolutely strive
to work in harmony with you and him
to serve the common good.

(*Trauta goes out.*)

And yet a strange cold chill stands by me here.

(*End of scene*)
(*End of Act VII*)

25) Open Temple

(The spiritual temple, which burned on earth, now reappearing in the realm of life. The Temple is domed and enclosed, leaving plenty of space around it and above it. Lucifer and Ahriman at first. Joanna, Barbara Finn and her child, then the spirit of Troy. Later, Marcus, Robert, Capstone and Meaghan. Then Benedictus, Stella Sophia, Stratham and Celia appear above. Also Blythe, Raymond, Thea and George. Finally, the Soul Forces, first Luna and later the Other Philia, Philia and Astrid.)

(Ahriman and Lucifer enter.)

LUCIFER
Now banished is the Lord of all desires
from this dread place transmuted here by fire,
the Temple built by Benedictus and his pupils.
It burned on earth and now is purified
and lives on here in ether worlds.
Benedictus has turned the Archangels
and their Hierarchies we had gained,
back to the help of human beings and seeks
an altar built on earth that stands in heaven.
But now, my comrade in the battle, you must
make sure this place does not become that altar.
Scattered on earth in their next life, the souls
who once were Benedictus' pupils seek to
meet one another in this place again,
to open it to all humanity
and welcome souls who gain their spirit sight in freedom.
This cannot be.
This must not be.
I had distracted them with pride and with
illusion, for a time. But now I can
no longer hold them back. They see me well.
And so I must depart.
But you, my brother Ahriman, can still
deceive the one indebted for her book.
She does not see how you work in her thoughts.

So now you can remain here undetected.
Capture this place and hold these souls
within it in your power.
Then I can blind them with the bliss of oneness.

(*Lucifer exits upstage right.*)

AHRIMAN
The time is fav'rable now for my action.
The cult'ral life on earth has fallen to
my influence; the law is in my clutches;
and those who think themselves enlightened
leaders of all humanity serve me.
They do not recognize that all their works,
which they intend to care for human needs,
dim the awareness of my influence
and help me dampen all the human sparks
that one day could destroy me.
These sparks are kindled here within this Temple.
But I will hammer hard and petrify it,
for if I can deceive the souls who come here,
all earthly spirit work will then be mine.
There will be no place left that can oppose me.
Soon I myself will live in human form
and lead all earthly culture into darkness.
Joanna, Marcus, Barbara Finn are mine.
Through them I'll capture all the others.
And the experiment in human love
and freedom finally will end.

(*Ahriman conceals himself. Joanna, Barbara Finn and Barbara's child enter from below, perhaps from the audience.*)

JOANNA
This place seems distantly familiar to me.
Within the domes above, such colors weaving
figures of long past epochs of the earth.
And there in colored glass,
beings of so many tales,
rising and working in the play of life.

The surging, growing forms
of walls and cornices and pillars
are not like anything I've seen in sense existence.

BARBARA
From dark depths,
grappling with enigmatic demons,
my own human folly
has shown me to the light
and let me find my way
into this temple.

JOANNA
It seems to me, the heights of spirit here surround us
as if descended to us from above.
I feel that I can only enter here
with deepest reverence and humility.

BARBARA
Within my inner life I have
seen many temples in the spirit realm.
But none like this.
This now seems closer to the earth than when
I've ever stood within such walls before.
All other temples I have seen were offered
from the gods unto humanity.
Is this the first one to be offered
by human beings to the gods?

See how my little child here at my side
can also feel at home within this place.

(*Troy emerges in a cloud of smoke or dust from the urn.*)

But, look – – how
mysteriously among the Temple's forms
our friend appears. Your brother –
as if appearing from below,
from death – alive in spirit.

TROY
This temple's monument on earth
is like a grave, a tomb. And here in spirit,
all its forms and gestures,
the images upon its windows and its domes
are livingly upheld.

JOANNA
What was the way that brought you here?

TROY
I struggle up from wrestling in the depths
and seek to clothe the naked will of demons
in thoughts and language we can understand.
I sense the beings in the earth
and wish to think the earth's own thoughts
within my human head;
I drink the air's pure life,
transforming earthly powers into human feeling.

BARBARA
As long as those on earth will only listen
to those who are unwilling to perceive
and to embrace the beings
living in the depths, and do not wish
to hear proclaimed the secrets of the demons,
so long will their own true spirit source
remain obscured to them.

TROY
I gather, Bobby, from your words
that you believe the time is just beginning,
when ordinary human beings –
as flawed, imperfect priests and hierophants –
initiate each other into th' light
of wisdom, through encount'ring one another
in joy and pain of work and daily life.
And now we've joined together – in fraternal friendship
with individuals who celebrate

renewing Christian rituals –
to bring forth fruitful harvest
in many human souls throughout the world.

JOANNA
Within this temple's domes
and firm, protecting walls,
the human heart can marry light to knowledge.

BARBARA
Look, now above:
These firm, protecting walls are opening.
Someone is coming in.

MARCUS (*On a ladder, looking down from above*)
Troy, I have found you here.
I had to lose my strength
as long as my soul did not wish
that light be joined with love.
You span the worlds that I had held apart.
Our work can be united once again.
Without your warmth of love,
I could not shine my light of love.
For through your warmth, you've granted power
unto the spirit of love
to give my soul-light to the world.

TROY
If I could be of service in this way,
it only is because
I could allow *your* light to shine
into the warmth and fullness of my heart.
And now I know the secret that can bridge
what has been held apart. What once was held
within this altar's safe enclos-ed space,
shines now in clearest light, in world expanses,
for all humanity.

(*Robert Finn enters.*)

BARBARA
Robert! You are here. The time has come.

AHRIMAN
(*Still invisible and inaudible to the souls.*)
Yes. Come in. Come in! And welcome to this place.

ROBERT
This sanctuary is somehow quite familiar.
The creatures peopling my stories feel
at home in such a place.
They are reflected here in images
and in their very essence.

(*Capstone peers in through an opening between the columns.*)

TROY
Michael.

CAPSTONE
Troy! You are here? How is it I could find you here?

TROY
Though I have parted from my earthly body,
I still may meet you here to work with you.
So we can find each other once again
and truly know the cosmic human temple
of which this place is but an image.
Just as a footprint in the sand
lasts only for a time
as evidence of th' one who walks,
so is this Temple evidence
of one that stands eternally in spirit.

CAPSTONE
This is the place I dreamed about.
The temple that was burned.
(*He steps farther in.*)

Unknowingly I've come here often,
with many who have come together
in communion with the Risen One.
We've gathered here in spirit in our quest
to be with Him and to unite ourselves with Him.
But only now I realize that this holy place
once stood on earth,
just as our Lord once walked and worked in life
among humanity.

AHRIMAN
These words ring here and scorch my ears.
The light shines bright here and it burns me.
And yet I will hold on with all my might.
Darkness must reign. This place must stay enclosed.

CAPSTONE (*not aware of Ahriman*)
And yet, what's happ'ning here?
It seems that some foreboding darkness
is unexpectedly pervading us.

BARBARA
How strange that in a moment of such joyous
recognition, – –
the air can suddenly seem cold and dead,
as if we're in a crypt.

JOANNA
Perhaps a moment's quiet stillness –
if we but wait in equanimity –
will then reveal to us what we must do.
(*A moment's pause*)

ROBERT
Our circumstances here release
a mystifying picture from my heart.
I could perhaps describe it to you
in a little story . . .

CAPSTONE
Please do, dear friend!
We long for the refreshment
that flows out of your spirit treasury.

ROBERT
So be it . . .
Once upon a time there was a princess who was cursed,
for any living thing she touched would die.
And even her beloved prince,
although he still was young, fell dead,
enchanted by the spell that struck him through her touch.
Now many came from far and wide
to help the princess's beloved fallen prince:
three lovely handmaids of the princess,
a snake, two flames, an old man with a lamp,
a woman with a basket,
a canary, pug dog and a hawk.
The snake now arched herself across the river.
The basket bore the prince's body
across this magic bridge
and all these folk and creatures followed.
The princess touched the snake
and, at the same time, her beloved prince.
The snake transformed
into a thousand precious stones.
The spell was broken and the curse reversed.
The prince sat up and stood and walked –
and yet his eyes were dull: for now he slept.
The whole procession found its way
into a temple made of rock,
which stood beneath the ground.
The temple then began to quake
and through the earth it moved,
breaking through stone beneath the river bed.
It then arose upon the other side.
Now there beside the river stood
a little wooden hut
in which there lived a ferryman

who carried folk across the river in his boat.
And as the temple rose up through the ground,
the little wooden hut crashed down,
descending from above, into the temple.
It now enclosed the prince,
the old man and the ferryman.
The three were trapped inside the little hut
within the sanctuary of stone.
The magic of the old man's lamp,
then turned the wooden hut to silver,
so it became an altar in the Temple.
The three men climbed out of the silver altar
into the large and sacred place around it,
and the Prince awoke.

AHRIMAN
(*To himself or to the audience*)
My ears are burning.

TROY
It seems to me, your magic tale reveals:
the time has come to step beyond these walls.

CAPSTONE
(*To Troy*)
But I have only just arrived
and found this place that I was longing for.

AHRIMAN
They do not see me here.
And so their might of thinking
cannot rob me of my strength.
I'll turn this place to steel and concrete,
confine its walls in matter,
lest it blossom in the spirit.

TROY
And many more connections now
are possible. The walls that once

enclosed this sacred place
are now becoming permeable.
It's boundless light shines forth now from beyond.
What radiated once
out of this central temple of the Sun,
the light of human soul-life,
rays in now from encircling spheres
of the periphery.
This temple's turning inside out.

AHRIMAN
(*in a powerful whisper*)
So work, condensing forces,
and mechanize, Satanic spirits,
the realm of earth,
with forces of your master;
to pave the way
that Ahriman's dominion can prevail
and, as my pain demands,
all shall obey my will.

BARBARA
Now look. Even as we speak,
these walls begin to change –
shining with dull luster –
the wood is turning into stone and steel.
It's coldness chills...

(*Meaghan now slips in, unseen by Ahriman. The area around and above the Temple is gradually becoming illumined. Michaél and Benedictus and Stella Sophia become visible above the temple, as if standing over an altar – as if the Temple* is *an altar in a much larger surrounding Temple space, which is in reality the entire cosmos. Thea, Raymond, Blythe, and George and Stratham and Celia are also there.*)

TROY
The grave is empty.
Come forth... step out.
Climb out into the light.
The air around us is rejoicing.

AHRIMAN
Hold, hold! Preserve this place.

TROY (*to Michael Capstone*)
Oh, Michael. Help us. Lead us out,
into the cosmic temple. −

AHRIMAN
Close the doors and lock them.
The ceremony now begins.

(*The light inside the temple goes dark − and/or it contracts with the eight persons inside it − so that we now see it as an altar within the much larger cosmic-temple space where the next part of the scene takes place. Michaél stands as Guardian high above, upstage center, Benedictus and Stella Sophia nearby; below and in front of them, Celia with Stratham beside and somewhat in front of her; Blythe stands or hovers in the East, Raymond in the West, Thea in the South, George in the North.*)

MICHAÉL
You, Benedictus, have approached
the beings of my time and age as
no human being has ever done before.
And your entreaty has been answered.
For generations, chaos has
wrought havoc in the karmic weaving of
the threads of destiny, which now begin
to sound and weave again in harmony,
for human beings living on the earth
have willed to find their way and hear my call.

STELLA SOPHIA
What has been held in darkness, you have found.
By many souls it will be known and seen.
And this seed temple will bear fruit for all
in times of deepest darkness yet to come,
if those who built its outer form on earth −
who suffered through its sacred conflagration −
emerge and work together once again.

The book of cosmic destiny proclaims:
that harmony of spirits may achieve
what each alone could never bring about.
Together you have found the altar, which
we build continually in spirit realms
from substance of our own souls' suffering.
And spirit life will blossom on the earth
the more the powers of vision waken you.

MICHAÉL
Your pupils once renewed
ancient sacred custom
within this place's counterpart on earth.
They each unlocked their souls
in their own way,
in order to receive the spirit light
according to their destiny.
The powers they had conquered for themselves
and rendered fruitful for each other,
forming a higher unity
to build that sacred place,
chaos and disharmony
of measure and of number rent apart.
But now the grace of gods is shining here
upon its seed potential for the future.

BENEDICTUS
A knot is loosed that once was tied among us
from threads that karma spun in world becoming.
This altar once made visible
the spirit realms and epochs of becoming.
Before it was consumed by flames,
it stood upon the earth.
And yet it only was an outer symbol
of the dome of stars,
the planetary pillars,
the earth foundations
of this *eternal* Temple in the spirit, (*above and around*)
in realms where Michaél
as countenance of Christ holds sway.

MICHAÉL
The grave becomes an altar –
It stands and grows within eternity.
The power of love offers
at this soul-altar of humanity,
within each present moment and in time
that cycles from beyond eternity,
in distant worlds and in earthly nearness.

CELIA
Wherever people gather on the earth
in love-filled seeking for the truth,
this holy place is manifest.

STRATHAM
May Michaél's inviting gesture draw us
toward what will be, toward what must come about,
that his sun-radiant robe of light
become a wave of words, Christ's words.
Then the words of the world can transform
the world Logos into the Logos of humanity.
Oh tireless friends, may you hear this vital call.
Receive this word of love
into your soul's dynamic aims.
For in our hearts we hold what once we lost –
the sacred words we spoke when we first entered
this Temple's ancient counterpart on earth.

RAYMOND
From the Devine Ground of All Being,
the human soul entered into earth existence.

THEA
In the living, forming Cosmic Word,
Death's dominion becomes life's revelation.

BLYTHE
In angelic Cosmic Thoughts,
the human soul will waken spirit.

RAYMOND
May the world Conscience,
resounding in the heights,
echo in depths of soul.
And Fate be remembered,
from cosmic space,
in active human limbs.
Then strength of will
lives in one's own I.

THEA
May dynamic movement
flame forth from East to West.
And guiding powers live
through rhythms of time
in tranquil spirit-meditating souls,
in beating human hearts and breathing lungs.
Then, in human soul-life weaving,
their I unites with the I of the world.

BLYTHE
May archangels bear aloft
what human souls wrest from the depths.
And principalities stream light from eternity
to poised, beholding, peaceful heads.
Then freely thinking souls will sense
the goals of gods in active willing.

STRATHAM
What I have wrought from realm of Ahriman
shall only flow into humanity
through service to the Christ,
the true image of the human being,
calling from future aims.

RAYMOND
(*To Stratham.*) Science, technology, psychology
will be imbued with human spirit working.

CAPSTONE
(*His voice heard from within the dark altar*)
With new-found strength in earthly body senses,
I now stand firmly in the flow of life.
I will work closely with this other soul (*Joanna*)
who has been close to me in other lives.
The Christ shall guide our way to serve and nourish
development of body, soul and spirit
of children, now and for the times to come.

THEA
(*To Capstone*)
History, art, nutrition, education,
will surge with human deeds of world evolving.

JOANNA
(*Also unseen from within the dark altar*)
United in this place in spirit realms,
and also in our earthly work together,
in harmony with world authority,
we'll serve humanity.

AHRIMAN
I still find access to this soul
whom I've stirred up tenaciously.

BLYTHE
(*To Joanna.*)
Humanity will unfold
religion, law and medicine,
from the eternal springs of cosmic thought,
to ward off earthly evils.

JOANNA
In humble resoluteness I will strive
to work in harmony with those
to whom I'm bound through many earthly lives.
Together we will serve the common good.

AHRIMAN
She does not recognize me here;
I still can influence her work,
and so she will not cause me painful terror
when, at her side, I use my power.

(*The etheric Temple now becomes visible again, and the surrounding space recedes.*)

BARBARA
From cosmic distances, I dimly hear a calling.
Three powers have dominion in the world:
The golden light of wisely thinking head;
The silvery warmth of loving heartfelt beauty
The brazen will of weighty strength of limbs.

JOANNA
The fourth is Love.

BARBARA
Love educates us, forms and guides unendingly.
It does not give us power over one another,
but power with each other,
to strive and work together faithfully
with hope, that we may draw forth from each other
what each could never bring about alone.

TROY
And yet it's not enough to love, one also has to see.

AHRIMAN
(*aside to audience*)
I can stay silent not a moment longer.
I must speak.
(*He disguises himself as Benedictus and appears.*)

JOANNA
Oh, Benedictus, our great teacher.
You come once more,

you who've accompanied my work.
I've waited patiently for further clarity
about the messages you brought
when you appeared to me within the church.
Now here within this spirit temple,
I'll listen carefully to what you have to say.

AHRIMAN
Dear children, I have called you here
in order to rededicate this building we have built.
I can reveal to you what spirit realms
wish to confide for your own good
and for your mystic path.
Within this Temple's monument –
its memory on earth –
you shall establish and maintain
a center for our work.
Endowed with power of the world,
you now can carry out our work
with full authority.

MARCUS
This sounds a lot like something I have said,
and yet it's not quite what I meant.

TROY
You speak about authority.
Are you indeed our teacher, Benedictus?

MEAGHAN
Who *are* you, and whom do you serve?

JOANNA
I thought that this was Benedictus,
who has so often guided me.
My vision's clouded in a fog –
I cannot see him clearly.

ROBERT
Tell us who you are.

AHRIMAN
When any being appears
to help you on the spirit path,
what need is there to ask from whence he comes?
Truth is surely what you seek.
So any stranger spirit-entity
that wants to do you service is compelled
to yield itself to service of the truth,
if you accept its presence so far only
as it is recognizable to you as truth.

TROY
We serve the good gods here,
and gladly will attend
to words of any being
who joins this service,
provided he makes known to us
his full identity
and gains our confidence.

MARCUS
Whoever you may be,
you only serve the good,
when you will strive, not for yourself,
but lose yourself indeed in human thinking,
thus rise anew in world development.

AHRIMAN
(*to the audience*)
The light shines much too brightly here. I'll have
to use my strongest powers of persuasion.
(*to those in the temple*)
I invite you to collaborate for the good of all.
If you will only pledge cooperation
with global governance,

your spirit science will become a part
of social life throughout the world.
All spiritual work in many realms of life,
in which you each now work and lead,
will be united and administered
within this temple's counterpart on earth,
supported by the power and wealth
of the whole world order. Each of you
will have your place there and your task
for world good. For then
all cultural life on earth proceeds through you.

CELIA (*illumined above*)
Joanna, my soul reaches out to you
from loving realms of angels filled with light.
Who is the stranger who is speaking to you?
I love it only when the worlds of angels
are willing lovingly to show themselves;
This being guiding the intentions of
the world authorities, is not like the angels.

JOANNA
Yes, I begin to see that for myself.

MEAGHAN
Our fellowship will always know itself
to be united with the God who lived
once as a human being on earth,
who suffered on the cross and conquered death.
We serve the Christ.
Confess him as your lord and savior.
The Son of God, Christ Jesus,
the Word made flesh,
Who rose from death,
and Who is coming now again.
Affirm you seek
to find his love within your heart,
and we, with love will then receive you
as herald of His glorious coming.

AHRIMAN
(*Losing self-control, begins to contort as in an epileptic fit, almost foaming at the mouth, trying unsuccessfully to contain himself.*)

It is *I*, not He. *I* come to you.
. . . That other one . . . is dead.
He is not risen!
He is not alive and will not be. . .
He has not come again . . .
. . . and even if he does,
no one acknowledges him.
And no one will. . . .
Curse . . . you! Cuh...

MEAGHAN
(*stepping back in sudden, horrible recognition*)

The prince of Darkness. Now I recognize you. –
For you once spoke to Michael through my lips. –
You are Antichrist!

(*Luna appears.*)

JOANNA
Marcus! The crucial moment has arrived.
Ahriman is now revealed in his true being.
Now call upon the holy solemn vow,
for it can take the strongest stand against him.

LUNA
Joanna,
do not allow yourself to be enthralled
by joy at your own ripened thoughts.
And do not let yourself be overcome
by doubt, which you can feel whenever thoughts
grow stale and old.

Keep all self-love and fear far off from knowledge.
Prepare your heart for sacrifice so that
your spirit only uses thinking's power
to offer fruits of knowledge to the gods.
Such knowledge shall become a sacred service.
And what you bring about within yourself
shall stream forth strongly to humanity.
(*Luna disappears.*)

MARCUS
Maria's holy solemn vow shines forth
an independent life apart from me
for those who can attain to it.
Joanna, use it well.
Break through deception that now clouds your thinking
and pierce through darkness to attain the light
that you can conquer as your own.
Have confidence in your own self and find
the strength and wakeful courage in your heart
to pluck this moment's ripened fruits to draw
from them their seeds for all eternity.

JOANNA
I will to open up my heart
to a true knowledge of the spirit,
so that, as humble offering to that God
who beckons gently from the future,
who is the Light itself,
I dedicate all consequences of my work
now and in the future.

(*To Ahriman*)
You wish to create world peace and order
by damping down the human spirit, to make us one,
not through the free uniqueness of each human "I",
but through a sameness, an "equality"
where it does not belong.

And when, in future, people read my book
and you attempt to use my words
to lead them all astray,
this holy solemn vow will answer you
with might from spirit realms:
the fruits that we bring forth
out of your icy realms of truth
shall serve humanity
through sacrifice of gods.

AHRIMAN (*to the audience*)
It is now time for me to turn away
in haste from this horizon,
before their sight can think me as I am.

(*As if to those in the temple*)
The time has come; at last my hour is here.
I leave now to descend upon the earth.
I will now fully manifest my power,
in*car*nate in the flesh of one great man.
I cannot stop your work. But, for three years,
while seeming to bring good, I will wreak havoc.
And I will drown you out. No one will find you!
(*He exits.*)

(*Gradually, the light begins to shine in from the surrounding Cosmic Temple. Stratham and Celia become visible again, as the walls of the Altar-Temple turn to silver, open and become permeable.*)

JOANNA
Ahriman, the enemy of good,
stood here in our midst
and flees now to the earth.

STRATHAM
And yet a form of thought he's left behind
proclaims in us the essence of his being.
He never gives up trying to confuse
our human thinking, since he still believes
it is the source of all his suffering.

An age-old error festers like a wound
that's seeking to engulf, and so destroy,
what has the power to heal. He does not know
that he will only be released in future
if he can find the essence of his being
reflected in the mirror of our thinking.

CAPSTONE
He does not show himself to us as
he truly feels himself to be.
Revealing, but concealing himself too,
he tried to utilize a favorable moment
in his own way, to strike our fellowship
within this Temple of the risen Word.
But now he can no longer hide his nature
from those of us who serve the spirit's work.

MARCUS
And we will vigilantly think him, even
when he holds sway within our inner sight.
We will interpret and decipher
the many forms in which he will disguise
himself when he must be revealed on earth.

JOANNA
Through light of our community
that spans the threshold,
we will prove strongly armed with power of thought
revealing our inner light
even at such times when
grim, bleak Ahriman,
by clouding wisdom, attempts to spread
his darkness and his gloomy night of Chaos
over our fully wakened spirit vision.

STRATHAM
It is ordained from world destiny that
this day must come.
The Christ once lived on earth;
and long before him, Lucifer.

Now Ahriman will have his time
and only then – if only people
recognize his power for what it is –
through having seen all three on earth,
will human beings fully know and claim
their true humanity. What must be, shall be.
And so will evil ultimately serve the good.

CELIA
From light-filled spheres around this cosmic temple,
a radiant angelic being appears
to stand with us before this silver altar.
And from Him words sound forth to us.
You also hear these words. And so they sound:

"What once the senses could behold
when I lived on the earth,
can now be seen by human souls
who've won a drop of spirit vision
and feel it deeply in their heart.
So now be comforted with sight;
receive new life through Me."

The Christ once lived on earth, and following
that life, embracing all of our becoming,
He lives in souls who seek Him in themselves,
through strength of their devotion and
through words His messengers proclaimed.
He joined himself in spirit with the earth.
And human beings can behold Him,
beginning only in our present age,
when He reveals Himself
to their awakened spirit eyes.
For souls on earth can be endowed
with this new power of sight,
as now the time has been fulfilled.

(*Philia, Astrid, Luna, and the Other Philia appear in a glowing cloud
of light.*)

OTHER PHILIA
From altars and Temples
are thoughts now arising
to cosmic foundations
of primeval worlds;
what in souls is alive,
what in spirits is shining,
soars up from the world of form;
and cosmic powers
bend down in grace
to human beings,
to kindle spirit-light
in powers of soul.

PHILIA
I will entreat the cosmic spirits
to uphold meaning for souls
with their true being's light
and through their sounding words
to free the spirit ear,
so what has been awakened
in human lives
on paths of soul
may never be extinguished.

ASTRID
Now freed from bonds of darkness,
I will convey
world-warming streams of love
to the anointed spirits;
so that the mood of consecration
can be sustained in human hearts.

LUNA
I will implore the primal powers
for strength and courage
to aid the will to sacrifice;
to change what times behold
to spirit seeds for all eternity.

TROY
O divine light,
Christ,
who once lived in the radiance of the Sun,
You who now live with us in spirit on the earth,
give warmth to our hearts, enlighten our heads,
that all that we achieve
with consciously directed will
may serve the good, through you.

(*Curtain falls while all the characters, including Celia, Philia, Astrid, Luna, and the Other Philia are still in the Cosmic Temple*)

(*End of scene*)
(*End of play*)

Lemniscate Arts presents

Anthropos'
Future Dawning

A new mystery drama
about Rudolf Steiner's characters in their next incarnation.
written by
Glen Williamson

A Readers Theater event
Sunday, May 15, 2016
10:00 am to 7:30 pm
Copake, NY

Performed by
an ensemble of generous volunteers from near and far
Directed by
Laurie Portocarrero

I have borrowed not only from Steiner's dramas and their fragments and sketches, but also from some of his lectures, verses and letters, transposing vocabulary, phrases and even whole speeches and scenes into new situations and characters. I've often carefully considered and retranslated the original German, but have also relied on Hans and Ruth Pusch and consulted Adam Bittleston, Harry Collison, Alexander Gifford, Richard Ramsbotham and Michael Hedley Burton and Adrian Locher.

Besides Steiner and Goethe, Novalis (*Hymn VII*), Tony Kushner, Vladimir Solovyov, Johanna Gräfin Keyserlingk, Aeschylus, Dante via T.S. Elliot, Shakespeare, Dostoyevsky, Lincoln, Shelter Somerset and Hiram Bingham have also been sources of inspiration, language, themes, images and situations.

When we read, play or watch Rudolf Steiner's mystery dramas, we know that they were written by a great initiate and so we look for and experience deep wisdom within each word and moment and situation. In order to write a mystery drama, one has to have a much more comprehensive clarity about what is true than do other playwrights. Where my vision falls short, I have had to rely on Steiner or guess and imagine. Of course I would like to think that I have also been inspired and helped by beings in the spiritual world, so that audiences and readers will experience something more, speaking through this play, than I have been conscious of. In any case, if I have depicted or implied something that is spiritually untrue or misleading, I trust that it will do no harm, since people know that this play is not written by a great initiate. Although it seems to have evolved into a somewhat coherent (and very large) whole (which was, after all, the goal) this project has been for me a kind of sketchbook of experiments and exercises. How much of what Rudolf Steiner was trying to express in his dramas really lives in me as my own knowledge and experience? Writing *Future Dawning* has confronted me with that wonderful and terrible question.

I am profoundly grateful to my friend Dr. James Dyson for embarking me on this harrowing journey. Of course we know that working together creatively, reading, acting in and producing Rudolf Steiner's mystery dramas is a very fruitful path. Who would have known that such a valuable probation could also be found in attempting to write one? I hope (and I know Marke Levene shares this hope) that more and more people will attempt such things in the future.

– Glen Williamson, April, 2016

Future Dawning
Sunday, May 15, Schedule

10:00 Prelude and **Act One**

Short stand-up-and-stretch

11:00 Act Two

Intermission

12:20 Act Three

1:00 to 2:30 PM Lunch in Café

2:30 Act Four

Short stand-up-and-stretch

3:30 Act Five

Intermission

4:30 Act Six

5:30 PM Light food break

6:00 Act Seven

Short stand-up-and-stretch

6:45 PM Final Temple Scene

7:30 PM end

SETTING

A community in the Northeast of North America; a church in the Midwest; the Monument and Archives of the work of Benedictus in Central Europe; various etheric, soul and spiritual realms.

TIME

The not-too-distant future and, in retrospect, the early 20th Century.

THE COMPANY

STAGE DIRECTIONS . . . . Laurie Portocarrero (Philmont, NY)

CHARACTERS OF THE PRELUDE:
MARY . . . . Roxanne Leonard (Mountshannon, Ireland)
TOM . . . . Tom Leonard (Mountshannon, Ireland)
THEIR CHILDREN . . . . Jasmine Lehrman (Harlemville, NY),
    Ermengarde and Hester Culley (Spencertown, NY), Eleanor Kress (Hudson, NY)

CHARACTERS OF THE DRAMA:
MARCUS LILLY (45) . . . . .Alan Thewless (Kimberton, PA)

JOANNA THOMASON (45) . . . . Laurie Portocarrero

SIMON STRATHAM (67) . . . . Patrick Doyle (Kimberton, PA)

CELIA GOTTLIEB STRATHAM (63) . . . . . . Julie Boothroyd (Copake, NY)

MARIO "TROY" FELS (42) . . . . David Anderson (Harlemville, NY)

MICHAEL CAPSTONE (50) . . . . Glen Williamson

MEAGHAN GERALD (55) . . . . Signe Schaefer (Great Barrington, MA)

ROBERT FINN (30) . . . . Stephen Steen (Hudson, NY)

BARBARA ("BOBBY") FINN (28) . . . . . . Sudip Peterson (Spring Valley, NY)

SPIRIT OF BENEDICTUS. . . . . Bernard Murphy (Soquel, CA)

SPIRIT OF STELLA SOPHIA . . . . Beatrice Voigt (Detroit, MI)

TRAUTA S. HARRIS . . . . Virginia Hermann (Spring Valley, NY)

DENIZENS OF THE SOPHIA COMMUNITY:
FIRST DENIZEN . . . . Beatrice Voigt
SECOND DENIZEN. . . . . Christa Macbeth (Chicago, IL)
THIRD DENIZEN . . . . Pete Lemire (Centerville, MA)
FOURTH DENIZEN . . . . Christian Peterson (Bridgeport, CT)

BOARD OF DIRECTORS OF THE BRIDGE OF CHRIST:
THEA TWIST . . . . Cheryl Martine (Lincolnville, ME)
RAYMOND GUMPTION . . . . Tom Leonard
GEORGE BATTLE . . . . Pete Lemire
BLYTHE TRUEGOOD . . . . Roxanne Leonard

SOUL AND SPIRIT BEINGS:
    AHRIMAN. . . . . Marke Levene (Freeport, ME)
    LUCIFER . . . . Sherry Wildfeuer (Kimberton, PA)
    GREEN DEMONS . . . Christa Macbeth, Beatrice Voigt, Tom Leonard,
                        Pete Lemire, Christian Peterson
    ARCHANGEL MICHA'EL . . . . Marke Levene,
                        John McManus (Pittsburgh, PA)
SOUL FORCES:
    PHILIA, ASTRID, LUNA, OTHER PHILIA . . . . . Christa Macbeth

PRODUCTION
    DIRECTOR . . . . Laurie Portocarrero
    EVENT MANAGERS . Marian Leon, Joseph Papas and Emily Gerhard
    PLANNING GROUP . . John Alexandra, Marian Leon, Marke Levene,
            Barbara Renold, Barbara Richardson, Laurie Portocarrero
    CAMPHILL COPAKE LIAISON . . . . Joseph Papas
    STAGE MANAGER and SCRIPT CONSULTANT. . David Fairclough
    SONG COMPOSITION . . . . Merwin Lewis
    SCRIPT PRINTING AND BINDING . . . . John Alexandra
    COVER ART . . . . Sophie Bourguignon Takada

Additional contributors to the development of this script: Brigida Baldszun,
Robb Creese, Martin Donnelly, James Dyson, Franz Eilers, Bella Freuman,
Robert Karp, Linda McKeown, Elizabeth Sevison and Mark Spinelli

This Readers Theater production has been made possible through
the generous support of the members of
Lemniscate Arts.

PRELUDE
A room in Tom and Mary's house.

ACT I (Scenes 1 – 4)
1) The Sophia Community in the Northeast of North America
2) A government office
3) Sophia Community and the Midwest
4) Church of The Bridge of Christ in the Midwest

ACT II
5) The Sophia Community
6) Landscape in the Midwest
7) Ahriman's Realm

INTERMISSION

ACT III
8) A cafe
9) Church of The Bridge of Christ
10) An apartment in the Midwest

LUNCH BREAK

ACT IV
11) Church of The Bridge of Christ
12) The Temple Monument and Archives, in Europe
13) Church of The Bridge of Christ

ACT V
14) Retrospective: The temple of a former Rosicrucian Brotherhood
15) Retrospective: The home of Felix and Felicia Balde
16) The Realm of the Archangels in the Spiritual World

INTERMISSION

ACT VI
17) The Realm of the Green Demons
18) Church of The Bridge of Christ
19) Stratham's meditation room
20) The Monument and Archives

INTERMISSION

ACT VII
21) The Monument and Archives (continued)
22) Finns' home in the Sophia Community
23) The business offices of Gumption-Truegood
24) Government office

FINAL SCENE (Scene 25)
Spiritual Temple in the realm of life

21st Century	20th Century	Fairy Tale
MARCUS LILLY	Maria	Princess, Lily
JOANNA	Johannes	Prince
SPIRIT OF BENEDICTUS	Benedictus	Gold King
MICHAEL CAPSTONE	Professor Capesius	Will-o'-wisp
SIMON STRATHAM	Dr. Strader	Will-o'-wisp
BARBARA FINN	Felix Balde	Old Man
ROBERT FINN	Felicia Balde	Old Woman
TROY	Maria Treufels, nurse, (the other Maria)	Green Snake
CELIA	Theodora	Hawk
STELLA SOPHIA	Maria's adopted child	Canary
THEA TWIST	Theodosius, Torquatus	Silver King
RAYMOND GUMPTION	Romanus, Trautman	Bronze King
BLYTHE TRUEGOOD	Hilary Gottgetroy	
GEORGE BATTLE	Gairman, Bellicosus	Giant
MEAGHAN GERALD	Business manager and friend of Hilary	
TRAUTA S. HARRIS	Ferdinand Reinecke	

A great big Special Thanks to
Camphill Village USA, Copake,
for so generously and warmly hosting this event.

Anthropos Celebrating our humanity.

Through the arts of theater and storytelling, Anthropos (*Ἄνθρωπος*, the Greek word for human being) seeks to uphold and celebrate what is truly human. Visit AnthroposTheater.com

Glen Williamson (*Playwright*) is a traveling actor, storyteller – and now playwright – based in New York City, where he has acted in numerous productions. He continues to tour North America and Europe with his solo epic storytelling performances of *The Incarnation of the Logos*, *Beat the Devil! (Faust, the* Whole *Story)* and *Kaspar Hauser: The Open Secret of the Foundling Prince* as well as with *Vonnegut, Vonnegut!* He played Johannes Thomasius in the festival of all four of Rudolf Steiner's mystery dramas, directed by Barbara Renold in Spring Valley, New York, in 2014. Laurie Portocarrero and Glen Williamson both trained in Michael Chekhov's approach to acting, under Ted Pugh and Fern Sloan, and have appeared with them in numerous productions of The Actors' Ensemble. They have toured widely together in the U.S., Canada and the U.K., playing multiple roles in *The Refugees' Tale* (based on Goethe's *Green Snake* parable) and in *The Gospel of John* with David Anderson of Walking the dog Theater, as well as performing two two-person plays, *The Mystery Journey of Johannes and Maria* and *Aeschylus Unbound*, which Glen co-wrote with the late film star and anthroposopher Mala Powers.

Laurie Portocarrero (*Director*) is an actor, storyteller, drama teacher and director. Laurie has studied and taught movement, drama and speech in the U.S., Canada, Switzerland and Australia. A long-time associate member of The Actors' Ensemble, Walking the dog Theater, and Threefold Mystery Drama Group, she has most recently been seen in *A Winter's Tale*, *Touch of the Irish*, and *Thornton Wilder's 3-Minute Plays*. Within the series of Mystery Drama conferences in Chestnut Ridge, NY, directed by Barbara Renold, she played Maria in Rudolf Steiner's four mystery dramas. Her one-woman pieces include *The Power of Imagination – the Life and Poetry of Christy Barnes, Miriam, The Path of Maria, Timeless Tales of Christmas*, and *Rise Up with Spring!* She leads the year-long course "The Art of Acting: Drama as a Path of Inner Development" through Threefold Educational Center. Laurie directs the summer children's camp Drama for the Little Folk, culminating in outdoor performances of Shakespeare on the Green for the local community. She teaches drama and storytelling to academy students at multiple special needs communities, and brings variations of her workshop "Drama as a Path of Consciousness" to conferences across the country.

www.ingramcontent.com/pod-product-compliance
Lightning Source LLC
Chambersburg PA
CBHW031056020726
47495CB00007B/1906